WHITE HORSE
IN WINTER

By the Author

Night Mare

White Horse in Winter

Visit us at www.boldstrokesbooks.com

WHITE HORSE IN WINTER

by

Franci McMahon

2015

WHITE HORSE IN WINTER
© 2015 BY FRANCI MCMAHON. ALL RIGHTS RESERVED.

ISBN 13: 978-1-62639-429-2

THIS TRADE PAPERBACK ORIGINAL IS PUBLISHED BY
BOLD STROKES BOOKS, INC.
P.O. BOX 249
VALLEY FALLS, NY 12185

FIRST EDITION: SEPTEMBER 2015

CREDITS
EDITOR: JERRY WHEELER
PRODUCTION DESIGN: STACIA SEAMAN
COVER DESIGN BY GABRIELLE PENDERGRAST

Acknowledgments

For those of my readers who know their way around a penalty zone, I am flat-out confessing that I bent some of the rules in relation to three-day eventing and combined training. My main eye was on the story, not on providing a training manual for the sport.

My deepest gratitude goes to my manuscript readers, each with their own qualities for spotting the flaws: Jenifer Wise, Randi Levin, and Linda Vance. Katherine V. Forrest gave me valuable suggestions for a revision which may have led in an unexpected direction. Working with Jerry Wheeler, my editor, was a satisfying and rich experience. I am so pleased he was there to help me make this book, as well as *Night Mare*, better.

I would like to thank Bold Strokes Books for republishing *Night Mare* and bringing this book to life, both in print and cover art.

Grateful appreciation from me to you for the support, expertise, creativity from Stacia Seaman, Gabrielle Pendergrast for cover design, Sandy Lowe, and Rad at Bold Strokes Books.

And last, but not by any means least, I would like to thank you the reader, because without you this manuscript would still be in a drawer.

For Linda Vance

CHAPTER ONE

"Aw, hell." I sank my chin onto my arms, stretched out on the warm metal roof of the car. I squinted, watching Jane's plane bank over the capitol of Montana, gain altitude, and line its nose up with the rising sun. Straight for Vermont. The small plane slipped through the space between the Elkhorn and Belt Mountains, and I felt myself shrinking along with the metal speck.

Love. Dammit, Miles, you sure did let yourself fall this time. Too much territory between our bodies, that's for damn sure.

A small, impatient whine came from Skippy. I slapped the dust from my Stetson with unnecessary force against my leg and walked around the car to the driver's side. "Move over, bud."

She did, quickly curling up on the seat and putting her long nose across my leg to look up at me with her mismatched blue and brown eyes. I stroked the silky light brown hair between her ears and felt a deep comfort that she loved me. One thing about a dog. You never had to wonder would they love you tomorrow.

Tilting the rearview mirror, I assessed the damage from saying good-bye to the woman I loved. My gray eyes were real pretty with red around them. My nostrils had matching red rims. In bright contrast, that old scar crossed my cheek. I eyed the bright white band of skin the sun never reached at the top of my forehead, and then I scrambled up my short sandy hair to get rid of the flattened bowl appearance from the hat. A real winner. Lipstick lesbian? Not.

I tossed my hat, crown down, onto the backseat, stuck the key into the ignition, and headed in to Helena. The grocery shopping didn't take long. My heart wasn't in my stomach just then. Didn't have a choice, though, since the groceries were sixty miles from home, and I didn't get to town that often.

A couple of days passed without a word from Jane. I had fallen hard for her after I found her sprawled on the dirt. The black mare, Night, had appeared at my ranch, and it didn't take a genius to figure something was wrong. I'd backtracked the mare with the help of my dog. Jane had escaped the horse van, which was transporting stolen top performance horses headed for new identities, by riding the big Trakehner mare into the mountains near my ranch. Her freedom had exposed the whole horse theft ring, and the Sandman, who could be hired to put horses to sleep for the insurance.

And now I'd allowed my heart to be vulnerable. Why on earth couldn't I just meet a gal who lived around here so I didn't have to struggle with Eastern values or have to commute thousands of miles for sex and companionship.

That evening, after a full day's work fixing fence, my brother left for the bunkhouse, and I dialed Jane's number. I sat listening to the ringing phone, but the answering machine took my call. This was getting tiresome. I shook myself and faced the fact she wasn't home. I'd call her tomorrow or the day after. Maybe I was too eager. What the hell.

Trouble was, a week went by with nothing. Not a call from Jane. One day I picked up the mail and found a letter from her, ripping it open with some vigor. It was all about shipping instructions for Night. Her identity search to find her former owners had come up blank.

A few days later, we loaded Night in a van heading for Victoria Branch's home, Jane's closest friend. The mare had a reputation for being a vixen. What no one seemed to understand was that with enough exercise and freedom, the mare was a peach. I again tried to call Jane and the same empty, hollow message greeted me. Right before I planned on hanging up and not leaving a message, Jane picked up, breathless.

"Darling, I've missed you. Sorry I've been so busy," Jane said. "I tried to call you over the weekend."

I sighed. With no contact, your mind could play "abandoned" tricks on you. "Norburt had his big campout, and I chaperoned."

"Did he have a good time?"

"Yes. And I enjoyed watching him run around with his friends. I'll have to see if he can have pals from the developmental school up here for an overnight."

"He'd love that. That black mare on her way here?"

"Yesterday afternoon. They expected arrival in about five days in Vermont. They're going to Saratoga first."

"Good. I'll let Victoria know."

"I gave the driver your map and directions. I sure do miss you, honey."

"Yes, well, I'll try to come out for a visit later on in the summer."

"You better, or I'll come and get you." I forced a laugh, not feeling a hundred percent like laughing. "Are you going to be ready for the rodeo? Have you been practicing with your rope?"

"I haven't had time. Things have been…"

"Oh?" Something in her voice worried me. "What's wrong, Jane?"

"I'm fine." The pause following this made my ears prick up. "When Night arrives, Victoria plans on boarding her with an old friend, Georgia. Well, she's more a childhood friend of mine. Vic is going to work the mare on Combined Training. Georgia says it would be a shame to waste the mare on pleasure riding."

"Oh. So, how does that keep you from calling me?"

"I tried a couple of times. The thing is Georgia has had some trouble at her barn. A woman she was coaching for the Olympics, Megan Fisk, died. Tragically. She's very upset."

"A horse accident, or is it murder?" I was only half joking. The long silence on her end chilled me.

"No, not murder. Or at least not her. Evidently, Megan injected her horse with some lethal drug, and the horse must have struck her when he fell. Killed her. The police think it may have been an attempted do-it-yourself killing to collect on the insurance. Megan was in training for the Rolex."

"What's that?"

"One of the biggest international three-day events in the world. A win there is as good as a slot on the Olympic Team." Jane's tone of voice transmitted amazement that anyone alive didn't know this.

"Why would she kill her horse if she was that close to Olympic selection?" That didn't make sense to me.

"She had a horse coming along in training that Georgia thought was better than her main horse. The insurance money would have gone a long way toward paying her expenses getting to the Rolex."

"I guess. People are sick." I tried to reason where all this was going.

"The insurance company is flipping out. They suspect this was something Georgia engineered because other insured horses under her care have died. It looks bad."

"If the woman who died was the beneficiary on the horse's death, there's no need to worry. What's the fuss about?"

"That's the trouble. She co-owned the horse with Georgia, so it's automatically Georgia's money now. She's under a terrible strain and needs help with the adult lessons. Megan used to do that in exchange for board for her two horses. That's why I need to be here for now."

"Is she gay?"

"What? What's that have to do with my helping her?"

"Do you want me to spell it out? Are you interested in her? Do I need to be jealous?"

"Really, Miles. That's ridiculous."

"You still haven't said."

"Of course not!"

"She's not gay?"

"No, she is. But I love you, and you don't have any reason to worry about my affections. She's very closeted, even to me. I personally don't get how lesbians can be closeted today. Especially in Vermont."

"Jane, I don't trust dykes who are closeted from other dykes. That's the darkest closet."

"I think you're judging her harshly, Miles."

"It's not that. We all need to be careful of queer hating. I've found that scared lesbians tend to lash out at other dykes. Like abused horses, you can't turn your backs on them."

"You don't need to lecture me, Miles. I know all that as well as you."

"Yes, of course you do. Guess I was ranting. But, sweetie, what's her problem?"

"I know why she's so closeted. She had an awful experience at Pony Club camp, when we were both young. She had a raging affair with one of the campers. A love letter surfaced, and Georgia's father stormed the camp, blamed the camp directors, Pony Club, girls, and horses, the whole works for sullying his daughter. He took Georgia home."

Jane paused. I waited in the silence for her to work through whatever she was thinking.

She took a deep breath, letting it out in a sigh. "Once, recently, we went out to dinner together. She got surprisingly drunk. I'd never seen her like that. She told me something I cannot pass on, swore me to silence. From the time she returned home, she had private riding instructors, exclusively male, of course. I've only briefly seen her at shows and events until a couple of months ago."

"The reality is, Jane, that many of us have had something like that happen to us, and we've gone on. Survived together. Queer hating is bad, no matter who does the hating."

"You can't possibly know Georgia's exact situation and judge it. Why are you lumping all lesbians together? It's up to her when she wants to come out. And I hate you comparing her to a mad horse."

I tried pretty hard to not laugh, but the sounds managed to filter through the phone line. "Jane. Jane, I'm sorry. I'm not laughing at you, just the mad horse part. You are absolutely right. Everyone's situation is different. So what exactly happened in Megan's death?"

"Megan and her horse were found dead in his stall. The horse died from a lethal injection. The syringe was in Megan's hand, and she died from a blow to the head. The horse's shod hoof struck her on the temple."

"This Megan must have been a pretty ruthless gal. Did you know her?"

"Not well. I've watched her ride. She was a truly beautiful rider. Most of what I know of her Georgia's told me." Jane didn't speak for a moment, and I listened to her quiet breathing.

"What's troubling you?"

Jane quickly answered, "Nothing especially. There are heavy expenses for amateurs—air transport, grooms, vet bills. She must have had sponsors, though."

"Is it remotely possible someone else killed her horse or her?"

"Miles, she had the syringe in her hand."

"She could've picked it up off the bedding, or it might have been planted on her."

"This is true. But who would kill her horse in the first place?"

Neither one of us could comprehend this. I dredged up motives. "A rival? Stable hand she pissed off? Somebody who hated her, or an ex-lover? Was she the sort of person to kill her own horse?"

Jane's silence ended with a sigh. "I can't understand why anyone would kill a horse. So I guess I'm not a good judge of that."

"You have a good heart, Jane. Part of why I love you."

Sometime in the middle of breaking that horse theft bunch, I'd realized how hard I'd fallen for Jane. I hadn't liked discovering this. Life had been coasting along just fine before she turned up on Night, a smelly package delivered express via horse van from Vermont.

Maybe my existence had been more like drifting before Jane. Now my body and heart hummed, fully alert. And ached, too. Well, I'd ride this horse as far as it carried me. Even though my experience told me horses could buck you off or go lame.

Our lives were so different. She was a Quaker with views I puzzled over. The death of her parents had left her a legacy of inherited money and a painful scar. Some wounds took longer to heal than others, but I thought she was making headway.

She was lucky she didn't have to work an eight-hour job. Did the work she loved, her newspaper writing. But there, we were the same. I did the work I loved, too, though the pay wasn't as good.

That afternoon, dark, full-bodied thunderclouds built over the mountains to the northwest. At the first crack of lightning, I scratched my outdoor plans and headed into the small room I used as an office. Once I'd written all the checks for September's bills and sealed them in the envelopes, I took a hard look at my bank account. Right now the balance was pretty low, but once the calves were shipped in October, I'd have working capital for another year. The savings book wasn't much better, but I could squeeze out a plane fare to Vermont.

I considered again the possibility of building a couple of quaint log cabins for dudes. Other ranches had successfully filled out the year's income by diversifying. I might even be able to attract upscale lesbians to the ranch for a summer vacation. At least two of the ranch horses could work for beginners, or the women could bring their own horses.

And how am I going to handle the extra work? My brain is already dull with exhaustion by the end of the day. And there's no money to pay anyone, at least not yet. Then I remembered me in Ag school at the university and some of the gals being so jealous that I could go home to work on the ranch for my parents, while they were headed back to Chicago or Seattle with no horses in their lives. Perhaps I could entice a nice young dyke Ag student to spend the summer and help me. I could see definite possibilities to that plan.

I glanced out the window and saw the sorrel Arabian mare, Alec, standing out in her corral, nose to the wind and ears up. The storm-driven wind lifted her mane, and her tail fanned out like she was racing across the hills.

She had come to me from the horse rescue organization.

She had been abandoned with only weeds to eat, and she was a walking skeleton except for her barrel, huge from the foal growing inside. If it rained like I thought it would in the next few minutes, I didn't want her out in the wet and wind getting chilled. I slapped on a hat, grabbed a slicker off the hook, and took off for the barn.

When I went through her stall to the corral, I saw the wind had blown the outside door shut, so she couldn't have gotten back in if she'd wanted. Made a note in my mind to put a sturdy hook on that door.

Alec saw me, did her weird chuka nicker, and half trotted toward me. I touched her on the neck and led her inside, closing the bottom of the outside door so she could see out the top. The wide overhang of the roof would keep her dry. I rested my elbow across her back, just behind her withers, and the two of us watched the storm come in, gusting through the sage with a moaning whistle that brought both a shiver and a smile to my face.

"Will you wait to bring that colt out until I get back? You look like you've got a month to go. Whoever would let a mare get pregnant to foal at the start of winter?" Of course she had no answer to that. I hoped there wouldn't be staggering vet bills along with this new colt. Alec had wormed her way into my heart and I didn't want her to die with complications.

I put a small scoop of oats and corn into her bucket, flipped a couple of sections of alfalfa hay into her rack, and ran back to the house. The rain felt hard and cold through my slicker.

I thought I'd ask my cousin Tess if she would come stay with Norburt for a few weeks. Sometimes one of the part-time workers at the developmental home was available to hire, but I never liked to do that. Hated to leave Norburt with a stranger because they usually treated him as though he knew nothing and let him do even less.

One time he argued about feeding the chickens with someone I'd lined up just for a weekend. He knew what to do, but the guy wouldn't let him go into the hen house to feed or collect the eggs. Now they had him down as "combative."

Tess agreed to stay, and I was relieved because I knew he was happiest when she stayed with him. I had to be back in time to round the cows up from the high country before the snow got too deep and big game hunting season began. Once the cows had been gathered and were in the low meadows, I had to start feeding, and that tied me to the ranch. The next few weeks were the best time in the year for me to leave. I bought a round-trip ticket, returning October fifth. That would give me two weeks in the East. The return date left me with a slim ten days to round up the stock. This Georgia thing needed to be checked out, and I wanted to see if Jane and I had lost our click.

CHAPTER TWO

My guts felt like lead as I shuffled through the security line at the airport. I hadn't expected the aftermath of the September eleventh tragedy to unnerve me to this degree, but I don't fly that much. I watched my one carry-on bag travel the conveyor belt through the x-ray machine. The alarm shrieked when I stepped through the metal detector. Everyone tensed up and looked at me. I'd emptied my pockets into a plastic tray but had forgotten about my ever-present jackknife in my watch pocket.

I had to leave my penknife in Helena, sealed in a brown manila envelope. An elderly lady had to leave her knitting needles and baby sweater behind, too. Then I recalled Jane's scent as I held her, drinking in as much as I could hold before she boarded the plane to fly back to Vermont. I felt the full kick of the memory, and yet it seemed lifetimes ago. How could the time that had passed be a mere four months?

Crazy. Now I was flying east to see if she still loved me.

Fighting back a surge of tears rising from my guts, I looked around the Helena airport to distract me from my memories. It had been seriously rebuilt after 9/11, taking on some decorator's idea of "the West." It had been a funky big room with a wing off one end for a café and the baggage claim. In the center of the big room had hung the Moth, a red airplane that had managed to land in a Montana pasture in 1829. All around the walls had been the stuffed heads of every game animal in Montana, their glass eyes fixed accusingly on the travelers. Always reminded me of Gary Larson cartoons.

Now all the animals were gone, victims of politically correct times. I suppose something was to be said for not glorifying animals as trophies. And the Moth had flown elsewhere. I missed the little red plane. The decorators had achieved some vision of the West—their own, most likely. Now the Helena airport looked exactly like the Bozeman terminal.

I waited for the other passengers to board, seated in the plane with my forehead on the scratch-fogged plastic window, watching while workers loaded luggage and gassed up. *What am I getting myself into?* Jane had sounded reined-in when I'd told her I was coming. The phone call came back to me in stabs.

"Why, of course I'm pleased. When are you arriving? I'll try to meet you."

"Try? Damn, Jane. Don't put yourself out."

"It's just that I'm really busy. Between this thing with Georgia and an article I have to—"

"Hey. No problem. I'll rent a car." I was so pissed, I'd hung up on her.

She called me back later that evening, and we'd sort of made up. I was still renting the car, though. Thanks to the round-trip ticket, I'd stuck myself there for two weeks, hoping it wouldn't be the vacation from beyond hell.

Well, I made up my mind that if it turned out to be a mistake and Jane didn't love me anymore and was gaga about this gal Georgia, then I'd go do something else. I always wanted to see the coast of Maine and, living in Montana, I never got enough of lobster. Deer Isle and its old farms and summer houses for rich Bostonians sounded interesting, and it was the jumping-off place for Isle au Haut, a part of Arcadia. I'd heard about a great bed-and-breakfast run by lesbians near Blue Hill.

I'd talked myself into thinking that this backup trip might be the better choice. All the maps and sightseeing folders were stuffed into a side pocket of my suitcase. Just in case.

❖

Damned if she didn't meet me. The second I saw her, I knew it would all be okay. Those doggoned telephones were no replacement for eyes, and hers held warmth and happiness at seeing me. She put her arms around me and held me tight and hard, bringing me home.

I rested my chin on the top of her head and let her warm every inch of me, and then I held her back to look at her. Curly auburn hair, soft brown eyes, and freckles all around a great smile. "You're a sight for sore eyes."

"And you're a balm for a sore heart," Jane answered.

I laughed with relief. "Guess you won't make me stay in a motel, then?"

"I changed the sheets."

"Wow. I'm honored. I've got that car reserved." I scanned the forest of signs looking for one reading *Car Rental*.

"You can cancel it. You're ridin' with me, pard."

I gave her a slow smile, and she took it.

"Is that your only bag?" She pointed at my carry-on.

"Yuppers. Traveling light. Look at that mess, people climbing all over each other to get their bags first." I nodded my head toward the clogged baggage area. "Bring me up to date on your life," I said, looking around at my surroundings. Too many people and too much electric lighting.

"You mean Georgia's problems?" Jane took my arm, and we walked down a wide passage filled with hurrying people.

"Yeah." I glanced at her. "Yours, too, I guess."

"I have gotten caught up in it. Georgia's reputation is damaged. Some of the Pony Club parents have pulled their kids' horses out of her barn. Her worst fear."

We walked through endless corridors filled with people who avoided eye contact. At home I never passed even a stranger without saying something or at least nodding. Usually it was by name: "How's Mary?" and Mary would say, "Fine. And how's your mother?" For me, being in the middle of so many people and not acknowledging or recognizing each other was lonely.

Then I realized I was seen, but it didn't make it any better. I noticed surreptitious stares and whispers behind hands, so obvious I wondered why it was done. Some kid said, "Look, Mommy, a cowboy," then laughed an unpleasant laugh.

His mother jerked his arm and said, "Hush."

I was invisible in the West. High-heeled cowboy boots, blue jeans, pearl-studded shirt. Here I was some kind of freak.

"You weren't listening, were you, Miles?"

"No. No, honey, I wasn't."

I didn't realize how out of place I would feel in the East. No one thought of women doing the work on a ranch. Trying to remind myself that dressing different and coming from a different culture didn't make me a freak, just made me a fresh change for Eastern eyes, I climbed into Jane's 4Runner. It felt like a cabin in a storm.

I took an even, steady breath, trying hard not to feel so relieved. "I'm listening now."

"What was all that about?" Jane said, giving me a curious look.

"Too damned many people. How far is it to your place?"

"A couple of hours." Jane laughed a little. "You have been on the ranch too long, haven't you?"

"I guess. I forget much of the rest of the world is pretty crowded. Oh, you know, I know it in my head, but my body doesn't until I'm in the middle of a bunch of people milling around."

"Are you hungry?" Jane started her rig and pulled into the flow of traffic leaving the airport.

"I bought a sandwich on the plane that was supposed to be roast beef. Must've made a mistake and grilled up someone's luggage. I swear I saw a monogram in there. I'll keep till morning, thanks."

Jane glowed in the slanting sun through the driver's side window, her hair radiating red highlights. She smiled, glancing at me a moment, and then she put her warm hand on my thigh. Everything was all right then: the beef-leather my stomach was working over, curious stares, and the Eastern overcrowding. And the months away from Jane. The hell with Georgia. We'd get Georgia out of the center of Jane's life. I wanted my gal back, all the way.

"Okay, shoot. Tell me the whole sordid saga." I hit the lever of the seat and shoved back to give my legs some room.

"I feel terrible for Georgia. She devotes endless energy to her Pony Club kids, and they love her. She's worked hard to get where she is, and the horse world can be so judgmental."

Poor Georgia. I rolled the window down, then rolled it up again when exhaust fumes invaded the car. "Well, a horse did die in her barn. There's got to be something irregular there."

"Georgia didn't kill that horse!" Jane put a fair amount of righteous indignation into her voice.

I thought about how closely veterinarians guarded those killer drugs. "How did Megan get that filled syringe, anyway?"

"Who knows? That stuff isn't left lying around. Once in a

great while, a vet will leave a loaded syringe with an owner if a horse is dying."

"What does Georgia have to say?"

"Georgia claims she had nothing to do with it. In spite of the gossip, it didn't matter to her whether Megan stayed or went. She says she bent over backward to help further her career—"

"What? Stayed or went. What's this about?"

"Last week the police were provided with a letter Megan sent to Georgia. No one knows about this except Georgia and the police. And whoever sent the letter."

"Who told you this?"

"Georgia. She said Megan gave notice that she would be moving her horse to another stable. Megan felt the horse would improve, work up to his potential under a different trainer. Georgia told me she felt that Megan's horse was not holding up to the pressure of competition. When she got the letter from her, she didn't take it seriously and shoved it into her glove box. Evidently, she'd forgotten about it. The next thing she knew, it had been sent to the police."

"Do the police think Georgia killed Megan's horse? That would slow Georgia's business." I shook my head. "Doesn't add up. Who took the letter from the glove compartment, and why would Megan kill her horse if she was taking it to a new trainer?"

"Good questions."

"So, the only reason the cops are interested in her is the letter?" I figured the law often had less to go on.

"Actually, the police are satisfied. Megan killed the horse, and the horse killed her. Perpetrator dead. Now the investigators are from the insurance company, and they're dragging their feet about paying."

"How valuable was her horse?"

"Threat Fear was easily worth seventy-five thousand."

I let out a low whistle. "That was her horse's name? Pretty weird." I said it a few times in my head. Threat Fear. Something about it nagged me. But Jane was talking.

"He was a Danish Warmblood chestnut gelding. Megan was scheduled to ride at Stoneleigh-Burnham School's event as a warm-up for Radnor, Fair Hill, and the Rolex. Stables training Olympic-class riders are very prestigious. Georgia wouldn't do anything to keep one of her riders out of the Olympic Games."

"If Megan took her horse and left for a new trainer, she wouldn't be one of Georgia's riders, would she?"

"That's true," Jane allowed.

"Did Georgia have other Olympic prospects under her wing? Any who might have benefited by Megan's death?"

Jane shot me a look. "That's way out there."

"I know, sweetie. Humor me."

"Ridiculous. Where are you going with this, anyway?"

I didn't answer, so she told me what I wanted to know.

"Naomi Bly, a very talented black rider from Atlanta. This is one area of sports where African Americans meet a lot of closed doors."

"Killing horses to open doors would be kind of extreme. Any others?"

"I don't know where you're going with this."

"Neither do I. Why was she taking her horse away? Do you think she'd had a fight with Georgia?"

"Georgia said they were good friends. Remember, she co-owned the horse with Megan."

I sat up straighter with a new idea. "Do you think they were lovers?"

Jane frowned. "You know, I've wondered that myself. No way to find out."

"Can't you just ask her? It could've been a breakup. What's Megan's background?"

"She's one of those girls who always loved horses. She bought her horse when he was a yearling for only a couple thousand dollars. Georgia located the horse for her and put up half the money."

"And he was insured for his full value?"

"All horses are at that level. He traveled to events on airplanes, clocking up as many air miles as most business executives."

"That must cost a bunch."

"I've learned she had sponsors who made her participation possible. I wondered about the suggestion she'd killed Threat Fear in order to pay her way with her second horse. She had enthusiastic supporters more than willing to go the distance with her. You know, I don't know enough about her personal life to know if she had other expensive tastes. Drugs, minks— that might have led her to do such a thing for money."

"It was all over too quick for her, wasn't it?" I looked at Jane, aware I was lucky to have her in my life. Wanting a long life and lots of her.

Jane reached over and took my hand. I held hers as the trees rushed past, and the air outside the window changed from car exhaust to the scent of mown hay and green leaves.

I was glad to see Jane lived in such a beautiful place. We drove through the small town of Putney in the dark, passing the wool and yarn shop on the outside of town and the general store at the juncture of two roads. We took the left fork.

Lights shining from the windows lining the street made the houses look like ceramic table decorations, the kind people set up during Christmas. I gave a little humph to see that these New England villages really existed. All this quaintness was like driving through a Currier and Ives painting. Lacy trees intertwined their branches above the road we traveled. The moon cast spider-web shadows through the limbs and across the road, which the headlights devoured as we drove.

Jane's car left the pavement with a bump, hit the corduroy of a dirt road, and after about half a mile, slowed. Tall locust trees lined either side of the driveway leading up to Jane's dark two-story house. I could see a barn, the hayloft door fixed open. A shadowy, white horse stood out in the moonlight. When Jane cut the engine, two horses neighed, one hidden by the dark.

She pulled up the hand brake and turned to me. We didn't touch, just breathed each other's breath in the dark and felt the warmth coming off our bodies. I got out of the 4Runner, walked around, and opened her door. She slid into my arms, and we stood quietly absorbing each other's presence, restocking the starved cells. A dog began barking from inside the house.

"That's Scout," she said, but we didn't move.

CHAPTER THREE

My body thought it was six in the morning, but the clock said eight. I stretched my legs down the smooth cotton sheets, listening to Jane moving around in the kitchen. No cows to hay, hay to make, or horses to shoe. No fences to mend, tractors to fix, or saddles to clean. I could just lie here and be indolent without feeling driven.

"What are you smiling about?" Jane said, entering the bedroom with two steaming mugs. Coffee aroma swirled into the room with her.

"Trying to get used to being waited on. That coffee?" I lifted up, shoving pillows behind me with my elbows.

"Hold on," Jane said, putting down her burden to fluff pillows behind my back. She shed her sage green terry cloth robe like a butterfly emerging from her pupa. I watched, mesmerized as she turned, light playing off the silk of her skin. The line of her hip traveled down her thigh, hidden by the edge of the bed. The dark hair at her crotch suggested a wild animal lived there. Breasts, full and round for their small size, with nipples the pale pink of new spring willows swung away from her body as she bent over the bedside table. She lifted one mug and offered it to me.

I held the mug two-handed while I watched her slide into

bed then pick up her coffee. I took a deep, contented breath and let it out on a smile. "Wish I could see a replay of that every last day of my life."

"If you were home, you'd be in the saddle already."

"Why, there's truth to that." The coffee was just like I liked it, strong and dark. I hummed in appreciation. After I'd drunk it down enough to be sure it wouldn't slop over, I reached under the sheets to find her belly with my open fingers, slowly sliding down to her wild patch, curious to feel if she was wet.

Jane pushed my hand away. "Get out of there," she said, laughing.

I put my arm around her shoulders instead and bent over to smell my fingertips. I licked them.

"Oh, you are so disgusting."

But I knew she didn't mean that by the look she gave me.

She set her mug on the bedside table and slid around, facing me. Our desperate, long-deprived hunger for each other's bodies had been satisfied last night. In fact, we had headed straight to the bedroom with Scout sniffing my ankles, fortunately not biting them. By the time we actually made it to the door, we were skin-to-skin, the length of our bodies. We lost contact with each other's lips as we collapsed on the bed, but we lost no time regaining the sweetness of that connection.

Now with the musky taste of good coffee in my mouth, I softly touched my lips to hers, the end of my tongue running along the edge of her opening. She parted her lips for me as a flower welcomes the sun. I wanted to touch her everywhere, allow my fingertips to imprint on her body so her skin would never forget me. Would always recognize my touch of mouth, of fingernails, of breasts.

I imagined myself without sight, my open hands reading the raised topography of her body, this valley of waist, twin rise of breasts topped with hard outcrops, the rounded knoll of hip, swale under her shoulder, and the moist canyon enclosing secret caves.

❖

Over fresh strawberries, milk, and corn flakes, we kept searching each other with words for the places our hearts met. The four months had gone by so fast when we looked back, but on the other side of those months, I had a long, hollow feeling of missing her. I'd heard that long distance relationships were the pits. Now I knew the truth firsthand.

Jane's little Norwich terrier, Scout, came wiggling in from outdoors. We hit it off right from the start. I was more used to the silky coat of a border collie, so her wiry one felt strange under my hand.

"How long have you had her? She's a cutie." Normally, I didn't like small dogs. They tended to yap. This one seemed to be a big dog in a small suit.

"I got her from the Humane Society three years ago. She was a throwaway. The owners said she tore up the house, chewed everything in sight. When I got her, I kept her in a crate in the barn so she could get to know the horses. That way, she'd never be alone and wouldn't have the habit of destroying things. I took her on rides along old logging roads, and before I knew it, she became a good dog."

"It's a rare dog that does well without lots of exercise." Scout looked up at me, bright and eager for life. "That was Night's problem. Too much stall time."

"Want to meet my horses?" Jane said, rinsing the two bowls.

"You bet. Show me the works. I want to see everything about where you live so I can imagine you here when I'm home." Saying this caused a stab in my gut. Scout jumped to her feet, her pert ears and dark brown eyes fixed on our movements.

"This house was built in 1710," Jane said, leading me from kitchen to living room. A large fieldstone fireplace sat in the middle of one wall, with small-paned glass windows on either side. The ceilings were low, but the rooms had a nice sense of proportion. Soft earth tones and a large oriental carpet gave the room warmth. The house was older than anything built in the West. Even Charlie Russell's two-room soddy in the Big Belts was a youngster compared to this structure.

"Here's where I work." Jane led me into a space off the living room with French doors opening on to a patio. Her Mac computer was sleeping on the desk, a small light shining on the front. I looked at the comfortable chair and tried to imagine Jane involved in some project, intense and creative. I knew it would be a long winter, and I wanted to take away images of her.

"I'm surprised you don't have a cat. A warm body to curl up with on these long winter evenings."

A wash of sadness crossed Jane's face. "I did. I guess I was away on my Montana vacation too long. When I came back, he was gone."

"Oh, sorry to hear that. Cats do take care of themselves."

Jane pushed the French doors open and stepped out on the fieldstone patio. "My dad had this patio installed. He was the gardener. I'm afraid I don't live up to his standards, only giving it occasional energy. I break down and hire someone to help once in a while."

I was impressed with the orderly beauty and the variety of flowers and textures. Fieldstone walls varying in height from a foot to waist high formed the flower beds, the stone beautifully fitted without mortar. Iris beds in tiers lined one curved side, and all the spent stalks had been trimmed back. Chrysanthemums were in wild bloom, all in rust browns and yellows. Narrow stone paths led in two directions from the patio, one through rosebushes toward the barn. The scent of old roses hung on the air. We walked past a nice dog run for Scout on the way to the horses.

"How long has it been?"

Jane knew what I asked. She stopped and looked around at the gardens. "Over twenty years since the Lockerbie crash. I can still see his touch here and there." She abruptly walked on ahead. I heard her clear her voice with a little cough. "He would be very disappointed in me for not keeping this up better. Mother didn't care, but I do. She only fretted about the dirt he tracked into the house. She did love the masses of cut flowers he brought in, though."

All the years since Jane's parents died in the Lockerbie plane crash had only managed to soften the pain. Old hurts still lurked. To me, the gardens looked groomed to perfection.

A bright little neigh greeted us, followed by a low rumble. A red-bay pony stood at the fence, alert and expectant. Behind, with her muzzle on the pony's back, stood a tall, white horse. "This is Moon Glow, the mother of my gelding Star Dust. She's blind. And this is her babysitter, Little Joe. He is a rescue pony I've only had here for a few weeks, but they are getting along quite well. Dusty is at North Winds Farm so I can take some lessons from Georgia. Victoria's there, too, with Night."

"You need lessons? I thought you clung on a horse pretty good." I scratched the pony under the chin.

"It's for Dusty, too. He gets bored just plonking around the trails. And I love hacking with Victoria. There's also a lovely outside jumping course set up, and a terrific indoor barn with jumps. Georgia thought he might perk up with some cross-country jumping."

"So, when do I get acquainted with this Georgia peach?"

"We're meeting for lunch, then going out to the farm."

CHAPTER FOUR

By God, if I'd known how good-looking Georgia was, I'd have worried a whole lot more. Her body language spoke the dialect many young dykes in the world strive for in front of a full-length mirror. Her features were Anglo-Saxon regular, with slightly more chiseled nose and mouth than I cared for. Her fine blond hair was almost white and cut short with style. In spite of wearing too much jewelry, gold chains and rings, her whole aura screamed queer. If she thought she looked straight, she was fooling herself.

Her lips were edged with perfect white teeth, either assisted by an orthodontist or capped with cosmetic crowns as she gave me the full-meal-deal smile. She sized me up with glacier blue eyes, and they weren't smiling.

"Becky Miles, isn't it? How nice of you to visit Jane all the way from Wyoming."

"Montana. And Miles will do. I get away from the ranch now and then." I knew she was trying to horn in on my territory.

Jane's plan was for us to meet, have lunch, and then tour Georgia's horse facility.

We settled into our chairs at a café overlooking a wide river. The person seating us gave out enormous menus that threatened our water glasses. I turned sideways for more clearance, but jabbed the person at the next table in the arm with the plastic menu corner. After a vicious look from my neighbor, I put the thing down across my plate. The chair seemed a little woody and the legroom short. I just couldn't quite get my legs arranged underneath without crowding someone else.

I studied the menu, which seemed a better choice than talking. I knew what I wanted to eat, so I wondered, instead, about the big river. We were looking east and New Hampshire lay in that direction. I'd always loved maps. I'd started map traveling on our family globe when I was a little kid.

"I'm trying to think what that river out there is." I looked at Jane and lifted my chin toward the powerfully flowing water.

In my other ear, a voice proclaimed, "That's the Connecticut River, Becky. On the far bank is a different state, New Hampshire. You're in Vermont now." Georgia smiled at me as if I were a somewhat slow first grader.

I shifted my eyes over to Jane, every inch of me dumbfounded. This would be a long lunch.

"Are you ready to order?" a somewhat flat voice asked indifferently.

Georgia said to the waitron, "I'll have Earl Grey tea and seafood salad." She patted her midriff with a knowing smile.

I smiled, too. "I'll have the chili, a cheeseburger, and a hunk of apple pie. With vanilla ice cream. And a pop. Root beer, please."

After the endless lunch, Jane and I got in her car, and we followed Georgia's beige vintage Mercedes out of town and north to the highway. Her car was one of those '60s pagoda-roofed jobs, which looked very modern and racy back then. Today, it looked like a safe had fallen on the Mercedes's roof from a high-rise building.

Jane placed her warm hand on my thigh. "Quite an effort, eh?" She smiled at me.

"Yeah." I squirmed in the car seat, wanting to get rid of some of the squashed-down irritation. Being with Jane calmed me, though. She got me talking and soon we turned into a driveway lined with artfully planted flowers.

Right away I could see why they called it a facility. Wasn't just a horse farm.

We got out of the car, Jane lifting Scout to the ground. The dog stayed right beside her. Georgia met us as we exited the car, striding ahead toward the barn on the grand tour. The twelve- by twelve-foot box stalls were bolted-together two-inch oak boards. At about chin height on a horse, heavy metal bars four inches apart reached up to ten-foot ceilings. Posh little prison cell.

The horses had a trapped look in their eyes. I felt very aware of my freedom strolling past their stalls. I wondered how often they got out to run and fart and just be horses. My bet was they never were turned out in a bunch, to whisk flies off each other or chew companionably those hard-to-reach itchy places along the withers and mane. A pretty solitary way of life, being so valuable.

Georgia was doing the tour thing. "We have two working students who help my man, Arthur, with the work in exchange for board for their horses and lessons. One of the working students is fairly well along and helps me teach at the lower levels."

Curious, I asked, "Is that the same arrangement you had with Megan?"

This question brought Georgia to a full stop. Slowly she turned to me and said, "You might say." She held my gaze for a loaded second.

A young red-haired woman stepped out of the tack room, and Georgia introduced us as Jane and her friend. "This is Betty, my assistant."

Betty looked like a one-off from Georgia with slightly more softened features. She stuck her hand out to shake in a friendly fashion, somewhat like a yellow Lab. Lots of orthodontically corrected ultra-white teeth framed her syrupy Southern voice. "Glad to meet y'all."

I sure was impressed when we entered the tack room. It had a red brick floor and neat saddle racks with brass nameplates all along one wall. The bridles hung on another wall with their own nameplates. The well-kept leather smelled like nothing else in the world, glycerin soap and neatsfoot oil. Trunks and blanket racks ranged one area. It was all gorgeous, if you lusted for that sort of thing. I made a mental note to do something about my tack room back at the ranch. At least get rid of all those old feed bags thrown into the corner. Trap some mice. That sort of thing.

Near the sink a grizzle-headed man with his back to us worked at soaping saddles. Georgia didn't give him the courtesy of an introduction.

"Arthur," she said in a commanding, high, thin voice. He didn't turn around. If it had been me she spoke to that way, I'd have been damned if I would have either. "Arthur!" she came close to shouting.

This time he slowly lifted his head. "Yes, miss?"

"See that you clear the buckle holes on the bridles with a wooden match. At the last show, they were filled with solidified soap." Georgia turned to leave without waiting for a response.

I saw his silent reply. He watched her back with hard, narrow eyes, his lips drawn in sneer-filled hatred. He slipped his focus to me, and then his face closed into itself and he returned to his work. After I shut the tack room door, I said softly to Jane, "There's a guy who could kill. Gave me the creeps."

"Yes. I wonder if Georgia's aware of his feelings for her.

I'll talk with her." We followed Georgia past stalls with sleek horses watching us from both sides of the aisle.

"I don't know that I would. She'd probably just fire him." That was the end of our whispered conversation; we'd caught up with our guide.

"Here's the wash rack." Georgia showed us a tile-lined stall with hot and cold running water. A horse shower. My horses got a shower every time it rained, which wasn't that often. She opened a set-in cabinet. "Everything one needs for braiding a horse's mane or tail."

I smiled and said, "The beauty parlor. Wash and a perm."

With no answering smile, Georgia responded, "The horses need to be properly presented at our Eastern events."

I took a breath for a suitable repartee but was jabbed in the ribs. I shot a glance sideways and caught a grin on Jane's face and a shake of her head. I could be polite, too. I reassured her with a sardonic smile and a quick wink.

A young girl all suited up for riding ran up the aisle. "Miss Georgia. You're here! Are you going to teach us today?"

"No, Carrie. Betty will work with you." Georgia smiled with the first warmth I'd seen. "But on Saturday I have a special lesson planned."

"Jumping? Can I ride Jess?"

"Yes. We'll do some cross-country strategy. You can tell the other girls."

When Georgia turned back to us, she still had a glow, a certain softness about her.

Jane took my hand. "Come on. You have to meet my horse, Dusty."

At the sound of Jane's voice, an elegant white horse looked over the half door. Scout left Jane's side and ran to Dusty's stall, wiggling her joy at discovering a friend. Scout placed her feet on the front of the stall door, and the two species touched noses in a greeting. Dusty sent a welcoming nicker to his person. When Jane walked up to him, he placed his whole face against her chest while she scratched his ears. "I do miss you being at home, Dusty."

"How long will you keep him here?"

"Fall is the best time for riding, isn't it Jane?" Georgia butted into our conversation. "There are training clinics available, lots happening." Her voice trailed off, I suppose because we weren't rapt with attention. I waited for Jane's reply.

"I'm not blanketing him after the first of October and plan to take him home by the end of the month."

"Will that be enough time for him to get a good winter coat grown in?" I frowned and thought, *not for Montana, but it might be different here.*

"Oh, dear. He'll look so scruffy. You can keep him here over winter, you know, Jane. I can give you a break on the board bill."

"It's not about that," Jane replied. "I think horses need time to just be in their sweat pants." At Georgia's baffled look, Jane explained further. "Lounging around and not in a three-piece suit."

My darling Jane. My thoughts exactly.

Georgia's lowered and furrowed brow said clearly she hadn't a clue. Her facial expression changed in a flash to a pleasant smile when she saw me studying her. "You might want to see the outside courses. We have both a dressage ring and a jumping stadium, with cross-country jumps out beyond."

On this side of the two-aisle barn, the packed clay floor had been raked in a chevron pattern. I commented on how nice it looked, mostly for something positive to say.

"This is done every evening after all the stalls have been picked up one last time and horses bedded for the night. Makes for a nicer look."

"So sad about the deaths in your barn," I said as we passed an empty stall.

"Yes. Megan and Threat Fury were putting on the finishing touches for Fair Hill. That's at the end of October—"

I interrupted. "Please talk to me like I know nothing." I knew something of the sport, but I wanted her to not gloss over anything.

With a quick glance sideways at Jane and a tightlipped smile, Georgia signaled that explaining everything to this moron would take forever.

"Of course. Threat Fury was Megan's horse. They were a team." She stopped in front of a closed stall. "This is Wyatt, her second horse, a backup." Georgia turned, opened the top half door, and stood to one side.

A very large chestnut horse moved toward us, rustling the straw. One small window embedded with wire let light into the stall, gilding his coat. He had a hard-edged tidy star on his forehead but no other white. I touched his cheek, scratched the groove under his chin, and then put my fingers to my nose to draw in the scent of horse. Been away from it too long. Two days? He rocked back and forth on his front legs and nodded his head. "Looks like he's bored and restless," I said.

"Who owns him now?" Jane asked. "Could one of us ride him? Does he get turned out with other horses?"

"Oh, no. He's much too valuable." Georgia shut the top of the door, sliding the bolt firmly closed. "I'm the only one who rides him now." She reached for Jane's elbow to steer her away. Her possession pissed me off.

"Jane, I thought you worked here to help out. Why don't you know all the horses?"

"I only deal with boarders like Dusty, and the lesson horses in the other aisle. Funny, isn't it, to know so little about this side of the barn, the private horses?"

I was pleased to see Jane disentangle herself from Georgia's guiding arm.

"You were talking about Megan," I said to get Georgia started again. We walked toward the large door at the end of the aisle where light and fresh air spilled into the barn. Scout ran ahead. She scooted to the flowerbed along the path and peed.

Georgia saw Scout peeing and yelled, "Here! Get away from there. Call your dog, Jane. I wish you wouldn't bring the animal here, he might bite someone."

"She wouldn't bite anyone." Jane picked up her dog.

Georgia touched the top of the dog's head with two fingers while making some cooing sounds. Scout growled. I was as shocked as anyone. Except Georgia, who looked vindicated because the dog was vicious after all. She smiled with only her lips. "You will leave the pup at home in the future, won't you?"

Without waiting for an answer, Georgia clapped her hands and continued with her tour. "Ah, yes. Fair Hill is an international three-day event in Maryland. It's the one that'll put riders on the short list."

At my slowly raised eyebrows she clarified, "The selection committee's list for the Olympic Equestrian Team."

"Did she have a chance?"

"Megan was an excellent rider, and her horse was schooled and coming along nicely. But I felt he was not quite at his peak. Last year, Fury had a stress injury and Megan backed off on the workouts. That's when I found Wyatt for her and helped her buy him. She blamed herself for pushing Fury too fast. During the winter, she slowly brought Fury back, paying more attention to long, slow work as I had advised. Lately, I think he lacked a certain brilliance. I believe she might have been in the top ten, if her horse stayed sound. And this is international, mind you. Horses are flown in to compete from all over the world."

"As a backup, was Wyatt ready for this level of competition?" Jane asked.

Georgia laughed, short uncomfortable bursts. "She never asked me what I thought. But yes, he was."

I asked, "Who was her top rival?"

We stood in the open door overlooking the dressage ring. A black woman astride her milk-white warmblood rode through simple warm-ups. The way they moved together said gold medal, loud and clear.

"That's her," stated Georgia.

"Who?" I tore my focus from the horse and rider, aware I hadn't been listening. I saw enormous regret and sadness in Georgia's eyes. She tilted her head toward the rider.

"On the gray. Megan's rival, Naomi Bly and Milk of Kindness."

CHAPTER FIVE

H i there." A cheerful voice came from behind. I turned to see a woman leading a black horse I recognized toward us.

"Vic!" Jane said. "I didn't know you'd be here today."

"Had a lucky break at work. Someone canceled an appointment." She led Night, the big black Trakehner.

Getting a look at Jane's best friend, I had to smile. Some people just walk around emitting warmth and happiness. I know it sounds corny, but this was Victoria Branch: friendly blue eyes, blond hair on the stringy side, lots of hairs out of place, and a big smile beneath a long, narrow nose. We looked straight on at each other, knowing without saying a word that we liked each other. She stuck a hand in my direction. "You must be Miles."

I nodded. "You've got a friend of mine there."

Victoria put her hand on Night's neck and said, "Yes, a good friend of mine, now. Everyone's told me I've got to do more with her than plod around on trails through the woods, but we both love doing it so much, it's not likely we'll ever stop. I do some ring work, too."

Georgia stepped near. "Yes, they're making great progress."

I didn't doubt it, though I felt Georgia was a hint patronizing.

"I'm lucky," Victoria said. "Night already knows what she's supposed to do. I'm just a passenger, praying I get the signals right."

"Doesn't she look beautiful?" Jane said.

And the horse did. Sleek and brushed. Calm and happy. Obviously, Vic rode her lots because the mare would turn into a vixen if left idle.

"Are you going out on the trails now? Let's all go." Jane's enthusiasm could catch anyone. "Georgia, do you have a horse Miles could ride?"

Georgia's face was priceless. She wanted like hell to please Jane. She glanced obliquely at me. "I suppose I could find something suitable."

"Great, I'll do some warm-ups to give you time to saddle up," Victoria said.

Georgia turned to Jane. "What will you do with the dog?"

"Why, let her run along with us, I expect."

"I am sorry, Jane, but you must understand. What if he frightened the children or went after one of the horses? Dusty might be fine with him, but our horses are not used to dogs."

"Fine. I'll leave her in Dusty's stall."

"Oh, dear. Will she bark? I'd hate to have—"

"No!" And that was Jane's last word on the matter.

Jane and I caught up with Georgia in the tack room. Jane went for Dusty's gear and hustled out the door. Georgia gathered the tack for Wyatt and said to me, "You can ride Mr. Cat."

By the time I'd searched through those little brass plates and found the right ones, they both had their horses brushed and saddled. One of the working students showed me which stall Cat lived in. I got the lanky sorrel out of his stall, led him to where I'd left the saddle, tossed the lead rope over his neck, and began to brush him. He'd pick up one foot to step away, and I'd give a little jerk on the rope, "Whoa." He was getting the picture when Georgia butted in.

"Around here we put them on cross-ties." Georgia said this with a little smirk.

"Where I come from, a horse should stand wherever you put him." I was trying hard to see whatever Jane saw in her, but it was an uphill task. In mud.

Placing the saddle on the gelding's back, I stepped back to look. It didn't seem like enough leather. There wasn't a breast collar or a flank cinch. It took me a couple of seconds to remember how to lower the stirrups. Georgia stood ten feet away with her whip under her arm, leaning against the stall across the aisle, watching me. The back of my neck was hot by the time I put the bridle on him. No problem there; a snaffle bridle was the same wherever.

Except the son-of-a-gun didn't want to take the bit, and I nearly stuck my thumb up to his tonsils getting him to open his mouth. Georgia watched to make sure I had the saddle on pointing to the front and the bridle on without the bit between Mr. Cat's ears. When satisfied, she left to lead her horse out into the sunshine. Wyatt looked eager for some action. I figured him at a little over seventeen hands. Bigger horse than I liked to climb on.

Fourteen hands two inches is the cut-off between horse and pony. Most of my riding stock are around that size. A hand as measurement translated out to four inches. This was an Arabic measurement, similar to the English foot, designated at twelve inches or the foot length of the current King of England. I don't know which sheik's hand had been chosen.

That put Wyatt at a bit over five and a half feet at the shoulder. In other words, mounting him was a serious undertaking. I figured that was why there were mounting blocks in the East. But to be honest, at times I'd use a ditch to put a horse in or a handy rock to stand on. I found that every year I liked my horses shorter.

A chorus of children's voices called to Georgia when she mounted her horse. They were on ponies and horses in the riding ring gathered for their lesson. They waved and smiled. Georgia rode near the fence and spoke to them. She was animated, laughing at something they said.

Betty came through the gate and the children reluctantly left Georgia. A certain softness trailed along with her as she rejoined us. "Are you ready?"

The rumps of the big chestnut horse, Wyatt, and the sleek gray of Jane's were fading into the trees ahead by the time I got everything sorted out. Mr. Cat's ears indicated a generally sour attitude, and I was getting about sour to match. I threw a leg across the animal, wondering where the fun was to this little outing.

Mr. Cat had iron sides, and no amount of hammering with my heels made him walk any faster. Victoria reminded me of where the fun was as I rode up. She and Night were patiently waiting for me. "You got the pick of the litter, I see," Victoria said. Her smile was the kind that made your lips curve up all by themselves.

"Hard to shine on this horse," I agreed.

Victoria laughed. She knew the score. The horse felt slippery, and I fit the saddle like I was wearing a pair of shrunken pants. It's funny, I never grabbed leather in my big old roping saddle, but I sure felt exposed and naked in this little thing.

Both of my hands were busy, each with a rein, like his education was just starting, same as a colt. A finished Western horse neck reined, and it only took a touch of the leather rein against her neck and a kiss of pressure from your leg to turn in the direction you wanted. Turn on a dime and give you back a nickel change.

Vic told me about the long friendship she had with Jane as we rode down the old logging road. I found a special pleasure in hearing about the woman I loved from someone else who loved her and knew her well.

Our trail ride led through cut hay fields and old logging roads under maple tree stands forming a brilliant red and gold canopy over our heads. Leaves rustled beneath the horses' hooves. We walked along side by side, trotting some, but mostly I'd call it moseying. Every so often, up ahead the rounded bodies of sorrel and gray emerged as a different pattern from the vertical trunks of the trees. Wyatt blended with the fall colors, but Dusty was in sharp contrast and easily found. The two of them trotted on ahead.

I wouldn't have a better chance to ask Victoria something in private. "What do you think of her?"

Victoria didn't need me to spell it out or say who. "Ruthless. A social climber. Homophobic." She snorted. "Would you believe, in this day and age? Perfectionist. Her only saving grace is that she's so good with the kids."

"Don't hold back or sugarcoat it for me."

Vic laughed out loud with her head tossed back.

I smiled to see such a laugh. "She has a friend in Jane."

She nailed me with her eyes. "That's all she has. All Georgia will ever have."

I couldn't help it; her words brought a sigh of relief to my heart. Up ahead Georgia and Jane had disappeared along the winding trail. Good. I had more I wanted to talk about with Vic.

"You and Jane are so comfortable together. Not all gay and straight friends are. Always seems to be a tension between them. Does Georgia ever talk about being gay?"

Another big snort came from Vic. "No way, José. Not much of her shows to the world. Like an iceberg. With this iceberg, I'm not even sure there's anything below the water."

We urged our horses into a trot in order to not fall too far behind our leaders.

I looked at Jane and Georgia riding side by side way ahead of us. They were yapping. Not one word floated back to my ears. An open field burst into view ahead, sunlight bright and warm on our faces, loosening my tense shoulders.

"So, Vic, do you agree with the police report?"

"No. I don't think Megan killed her own horse. She loved Fury, was about to move him to a new place."

"Wait. How do you know that?" I remembered Jane saying that only Georgia, the police, and Jane knew about the letter. Could Vic have been the one who sent the letter to the police?

"She told me. Megan. I'm not sure why she was moving the horse, exactly. Maybe she found a coach who she believed could push her beyond her present level. Lately, she and Georgia were ultra-civil and Fury had no flash. I'd say he was listless."

"Really? How lately was this?" I was raging with curiosity. Nothing fit in the basic horse-sense way about this dual death.

"Actually, I think the strained feelings started when Naomi Bly brought her horse here. About four months ago."

"Naomi. Is that the pretty rider on the white horse? But I thought you just started coming here. When Night arrived."

"No, I've been hanging out around this barn for ages. This is the gathering place for Pony Club. Don't forget I've got a horse crazy daughter. She was bitten with the combined training Bug a long time ago. Now she's away at Stoneleigh-

Burnham School. That's a girls' school, which has a very strong horse program. I miss her."

"How far away is that?"

"Only an hour's drive. Might as well be in California."

"Doesn't she come home weekends?"

"You can't pry her away from her horse, her girlfriends, the whole place. Her academic work is better than it's ever been. Michael and I are reconciled to early, childless old age."

"Oh, it can't be that bad."

"Really? Occasionally, we get too lonely for our daughter and drive down to the school with the horse trailer. Bringing the horse home is the only way to get her for a long weekend."

I couldn't reconcile Jane's friendship choices with my knowledge of Victoria and Georgia. Two more different women didn't exist. I must have been missing something. I spotted our guides who had stopped, waiting for us to catch up with them where the trail ride would enter the dense woods. When we neared, Georgia turned her horse to go on and urged him into a strong trot.

Jane called, "Are you having fun yet?"

"Trying," I replied as we rode up.

Jane laughed and trotted her horse on to join Georgia. Vic and I got our horses into a trot, too. I had a much tougher time of it than Vic did. I think it was more Mr. Cat's separation fears than my heels. I saw Georgia glance back to see how I was handling it. A lot of people think Western riders don't know how to post the trot. They are wrong. We don't in the show ring but sure as hell do going a distance or over rough ground. I saw her disappointment.

Well, Jane might not have wanted to be lovers with Georgia, but Georgia wanted her. Any fool could see that. And she wanted to discredit me and send me back where I'd come from. Far-off Wyoming.

We came to a place where the logging road let out into a large, recently cut hayfield that invited a good gallop. At that moment, Naomi Bly on her massive white horse burst into view from a side trail. Naomi was strikingly beautiful. She wasn't wearing a safety helmet, simply a tweed cloth cap over her jet-black hair. What tickled me was that she wore her hair in tiny cornrows instead of straightening it into that cardboard faux-Caucasian look. The smile on her face dissolved when she saw us as she brought her horse down from a gallop to a walk in a few strides.

"Ms. Bly," Georgia said. "I'd like you to meet—"

Ms. Bly was having none of it. The white horse did one of those dressage rears, rocking back on his hindquarters, both feet tucked in front like a begging dog. He sprang forward into a strong gallop. They made a pretty picture crossing that dark green field, the contrast striking.

I thought about times I'd gone out to look for my horse herd. I'd look for the white one, old Jeff. Once you'd found Jeff, the rest of the herd was close by. Easy to spot him against the green or yellow grass or behind the dark limbs of the fir. Course, in winter it was another story.

Georgia's lower jaw sagged watching them. "Really a very nice person," she managed when she could work her mouth again.

"Doubtless," I said, amused at Naomi's snub.

At that instant, an explosion of sound struck us. Horses were jumping all over each other. They were spooked and blasting snorts from their nostrils, their ears riveted on a spot at the bottom of the field. Naomi's dark form lay on the grass, and her gelding bucked his way across the field. Jane and Vic took off for Naomi. Georgia headed in a direct course for the horse. I caught at a glance that the horse was lined out for a busy highway if he followed the trees planted in a curved row.

Every year a lot of horses were killed by cars. I didn't want this horse to be one of the statistics. I rode hell-bent for leather to head him off.

Georgia was not gaining on Naomi's horse. If anything, the white horse was running faster. I knew Mr. Cat could never run fast enough to get near that fit and adrenaline-charged animal.

CHAPTER SIX

Terrified horses don't have much sense, and you can never catch up to a horse without a rider. They just plain aren't packing any weight. But sometimes if they're running scared and see another horse ahead of them, they'll join up. If I could get Mr. Cat to go fast enough, I might be able to get into the panicked horse's line of sight. This was what I aimed to do.

Mr. Cat didn't want to go off in a different direction from all the other horses, and he took some persuading. Eventually we traveled at a lackluster canter, with me hammering his sides for more speed. Georgia's pursuit of the white horse increased his fear. By this time she was driving the horse toward me. His eyes rolled back, ears flicking to front, then back. His mouth flecked blood from stepping on the reins, breaking them. Pain and fear drove him.

The way everything was playing out, he would reach the highway before I could head him off. I began shouting, standing in my stirrups to get the gray's attention. He spotted me, and at that instant, I brought Mr. Cat down to a calm walk and then encouraged him to drop his head to graze. That didn't take too much work, as the horses at the facility never got any grass.

When I was sure the white horse saw us, I turned Mr. Cat's rump to Naomi's horse and slowly began walking away.

The sound of the cars and trucks on the highway was chilling. I held my breath listening for the shriek of brakes and the dull thud of a struck horse.

I let my breath out as I heard the horse trot up to us. He got close to Mr. Cat, then dropped his head and snatched a mouthful of grass, quickly raising it to watch the pursuer. He spun around to face the approaching rider and horse.

I could hear Georgia pounding up to us and hollered, "Stay back." She didn't, riding Wyatt right up to the nervous horse. Naomi's horse circled a bit, but he had already hooked up to Mr. Cat, believing him a safe herd. Georgia rammed into Mr. Cat, her horse worked up and not listening well to her aids. This collision alarmed the white horse and sent all three horses into a tense, milling mass of horseflesh. Still determined to catch the loose horse, Georgia reached out to grasp the tattered ends of the reins, but the white gelding jerked back each time.

"Give him a minute. He's not going anywhere now," I advised.

"Oh? Did he speak to you? Are you a Horse Whisperer?" The sarcasm glinted off her words.

"Yeah. Didn't Jane tell you? I travel all over the West, reaching into the deep and damaged recesses of horse psyches to heal and release them." I didn't give a damn what Georgia thought of me, all I wanted was more time for Naomi's horse to settle. After he'd grabbed another succulent snack of grass, I side-passed my horse close up to the gray, scratched the side of his neck for a minute, and then slowly reached down to take his broken reins.

Tilting my head in Naomi's direction, I said, "Lead off."

Other than dancing around a bit, the horse was over the terror induced by the sudden loud noise. I hoped Naomi was unhurt. She lay motionless on the grass. Jane and Victoria knelt beside her. When we rode up, I desperately wanted to see how she was. But someone had to hold the horses, and Georgia had leapt off and tossed her reins in my direction, huddling over Naomi.

"How is she? Is she hurt?" I asked, as I saw Naomi sit up.

Jane rose to her feet and came to me. "Got the wind knocked out of her. I don't think anything's broken. I was worried about the horse, and I imagine Naomi is, too. She was so relieved when Georgia told her she'd caught him just before the road."

"You don't say?" I couldn't help but smile as I dismounted to rig up reins Naomi could use to ride back to the barn. There wasn't much to use. On my western saddle, I had various straps and thongs I could detach, hobbles wrapped around the flank cinch, and little strings of rawhide for trailside repairs.

The nylon windbreaker I wore was past its prime, and I thought of cutting a strip from that. Without thinking, I reached for my pocketknife and had a jolt when it was gone. Then I remembered it was back in Montana. I asked, but no one else had one.

At that point, I passed two horses over to Jane and rode Mr. Cat around looking for something. I found an orange string of baling twine on the edge of the field. It was long enough to do double duty. Curious about the cause of the explosive sound, I rode Mr. Cat through the band of trees. On the far side was an automobile repair shop. Most likely a car had backfired. As I returned to the group in the field, I could see Naomi checking her horse's legs. When I handed the baling twine to her, she gave me a genuine smile.

"That was thoughtful of you," she said in a voice soft as humid air. "Did you find out why he bolted?"

I told her as she tied the orange plastic to the bit and then mounted her horse. Her hands were shaking like crazy as she picked up the mismatched reins, but her lips were firm.

I said, "Just your bad luck. Will you be heading back to the barn?"

She looked at me strangely. "Yes. Why do you ask?"

"I'll ride with you." She began to puff up, but before she could deliver a lecture to me on her ability to take a fall, I said, "I've had enough trail riding fun for today."

"I wouldn't mind the company," she said, a smile melting her face. "I'm feeling just this side of dizzy."

I hollered to the others, "Meet you back at the facility." My private joke. When I swept my gaze back in Naomi's direction, I was surprised to find she'd gotten it, a grin playing on the edges of her lips. We rode in silence for a while. The contrast between the athletic, beautiful white horse and the mousey sorrel made me laugh. I waved my hand at the two and said, "The sun and the flashlight."

"You're not like the usual person who hangs out here. This is not your element, and it's refreshing." Her dark eyes, deep and brown, showed humor through the surrounding tiny muscles. Lively and expressive eyes.

"No, can't say it is. I miss..." My voice trailed off, because I missed so much there wasn't one thing to single out. I actually missed the wind, the stink of the juniper, the hard work, and my brother.

"Texas? Or, no, didn't Georgia say Jane had a friend visiting from Wyoming?"

"Closer than Texas, anyway. Montana's my home."

"I miss my family. They're in North Carolina."

"Must be lonely and hard for you in this circle. There aren't many African Americans competing at upper levels in the horse world."

"If I'd known how hard..." She was silent for a minute. "I wanted to get to this level so bad. My dream as a kid was riding in the Olympics."

"Sounds like you're near your goal. Do you mind telling me what you had to go through?"

"When I was a little girl, I'd bicycle out past the houses in our subdivision to the place where pastures and fences were. Sometimes there would be cows grazing, other times horses. In one pasture was a team of black Shires. They worked as a team in harness. When turned out, they grazed side by side, their noses almost touching. I watched those gentle draft horses for hours every chance I could get.

"One Saturday my dad came looking for me because I'd missed lunch. I didn't understand then why he was so worried. He put my bike on the backseat and on the way home asked me why I'd been gone for three hours."

I laughed. "When I was a toddler, my folks knew where to find me when I wandered off—the horse corrals and the barn. The smells of hay and straw laced with all those body smells of horses." I closed my eyes and shook my head. "There's nothing more comforting for me in the world than the sound of a horse chewing hay."

Naomi smiled with her own warm memories. "I don't remember what I said to my father that day, but the next week I began taking riding lessons. Dad must have done some excellent research to find that riding school, because the place was good, the kids were nice, and there were even some other black kids in my classes.

"Best of all, the quality of instruction prepared me for everything I wanted to do on the back of a horse. Miss Trudy. I don't even know her last name. I was fourteen when my parents gave me permission to get some higher horse education. I found a dressage stable and called to set up an evaluation ride. When I arrived, the instructor appeared flustered, tried to turn me away, and denied I'd made an appointment. She hadn't realized over the phone that I'm black."

"Did you understand what was going on?"

"Oh, yeah. I'd been in that situation with countless variations before. I insisted on riding. The instructor said that I looked ridiculous on a horse. After half an hour of humiliation, she said I'd never make it and refused to work with me. I was just a kid. It was hard to tell if my riding wasn't good enough or if she simply didn't want to work with me. Then I realized what it was; I didn't fit the frame."

Her laughter was tight with years of pain and struggle, hardened like fine steel with her own persistence. "You know how riders are always referring to the frame? Fitting the frame. Well, I sure as hell didn't."

"Well, you made it fit, didn't you? Sent the frame to a woodworker." We both laughed. "I saw you doing your warm-ups and thought you were gold medal material."

"Thanks. I work my horse hard, but every day I take him out to run and have fun. He enjoys the trails." She patted his neck, her smile changing to a frown. "The person I met most often out here was Megan. I think we were the only two riders who knew how much our horses loved this time through the woods."

"Look," I said. "Megan doesn't sound like the sort of ruthless gal who'd kill her own horse. What do you think?"

This time Naomi was careful. "Honestly, I didn't know her that well."

Her eyes met mine, and I felt a frank solidness. It's like the way some horses look you in the eye, and you know they'll buck you off if they get the chance and claim it was the fault of a bunny jumping from the bushes. Others have no buck, and they'll play you fair. Hers were like that.

Naomi said, "No, that's not really being honest. I did know her fairly well. Sometimes on our rides, we'd talk with the sort of openness you sometimes do with people who live other lives. Our deep talks were sporadic. But kill her horse? That was something Megan would never do."

I nodded. "The things I've heard about her agree with that. Everything points to Megan killing her horse. In spite of that, the story's wrong, and that bothers me. I want to know why. And I'd like to see the answer fit the person."

"Yes. I know what you mean."

We left the woods trail and rode into an open field dotted with cross-country jumps. The sunshine felt good. Naomi took a deep breath of the sun-warmed air, then said, "I understand there was an indentation in her skull that fits a horseshoe."

"I think everything fits too well. There must be more to the story."

"Anything's possible." She paused as though something had just occurred to her. "Aren't you aware that Georgia and Megan were lovers?"

Whammy. "No. I didn't know that. I've heard that Georgia's deep in the closet."

"Georgia put the make on me. She figured I was gay because I don't have a man hanging on me every minute of the day. I'm not a lesbian. I simply don't have time in my life for men. Guess I royally got Georgia's goat by spurning her affections." Naomi made a sound pretty close to chuckling.

"The closet thing was the turning point for Megan, though," Naomi continued. "She was fed up with Georgia's sham of passing for straight. Megan actually pushed her to get legally married. But she grew tired of Georgia's lack of commitment to their relationship, her predatory affairs, and her possessiveness. Not to mention Georgia acting like she owned Megan and keeping her on a short leash."

"I understood things were on the tense side around here." Boy, I thought, I'd hit a gold mine.

"Yes. It wasn't long after Georgia's pass at me that Megan got a new trainer and was about to remove her horse."

Everyone, it seemed, knew about Megan's impending departure. "You know her name?"

"The trainer? Sure, Babs Longfellow."

❖

I pulled the saddle from Cat, released Scout from Dusty's stall, and led Cat to a nearby corral to roll. He'd done his best and deserved some dirt in his hide.

I'd forgotten to ask Naomi where Babs Longfellow was located. Before I pestered her again, I decided I'd look in the farm office. She wasn't listed locally in the telephone book, but as I stood staring at the desk wondering how to find her, I saw it scribbled on a clipboard along with a bunch of other numbers. I copied it on a scrap of paper and tucked it in my shirt pocket.

CHAPTER SEVEN

When we drove back to Jane's home and walked through the kitchen door into the warmth of her surroundings, I was struck by how much a home or a barn, for that matter, shows who lives inside. It's not just a matter of taste or how much money you spend to buy furnishings. It's what you choose to live among that reflects who you are. Maybe it is even more than that, like the whorls of your inner fingerprint.

What I know for certain is that as soon as I entered Jane's house, I let down. All my edges had been hard and ready at Georgia's barn. On guard.

"Poor Naomi. Did you enjoy riding back with her?"

"I did. She's an interesting woman. I admire her courage."

"Yes, she did get right back on her horse."

"No, not that. But yes, she did. I meant to even have achieved this high level of riding, to have had the grit to face all the barriers to her success and come out strong. We whites like to fool ourselves there's no prejudice these days out there among 'nice' people. But we're not on the receiving end. I've always imagined that racism and homophobia are sisters."

Jane gave me a long look. "So you did like her?"

What the hell did she mean by that? "Why, yes. Evidently, so did your friend, Georgia. Enough to make a pass."

"Is that what she said?"

"Georgia thought she was a lesbian because she wasn't with a man."

"I've made that mistake myself." Jane gave a little rueful laugh.

"Are you aware that Georgia and Megan were lovers?"

Jane stilled, letting the knowledge in. "No. I'd wondered at their relationship. Is that what Naomi said?"

I nodded. "Complicates things, doesn't it? With Megan planning on moving her horse, it smacks of a nasty breakup."

"Especially nasty if Georgia refused to let her take Fury off the farm. Maybe Megan killed the horse because that was the only way she'd get anything out of the deal. Half of seventy-five thousand is better than half a horse you can't have access to."

"All this points to Megan killing her own horse." My gut feelings didn't support that conclusion.

"That's true, but I never sensed that Georgia was angry or vindictive with her."

"Hard to tell. She made her moves on Naomi before Megan died, and she's after you now."

Jane reached her arms around me, pulled my slightly resisting body close to her, and nuzzled my neck. She kissed me with soft lips and said, "I'm yours, baby."

"Ah. Just what I wanted to hear." I took her in my arms and playfully lifted her off the floor. Jane gave a shriek and bit me at the base of my neck. For some strange reason, this turned me on big-time, and things got pretty hot there for a while.

The next morning, I came awake with a smile on my lips. I'd clean forgotten what it was like to wake after a night of lovemaking, your body soft and satisfied yet every cell alive with awareness.

Lying right in front of me, the cause of it all was gently snoring. I rolled on my back and stretched my legs out to the footboard. Damn thing got in the way last night. A sigh came from my right, then Jane burrowed against my side.

One word came from under the covers. "Coffee."

"Didn't you set up your magic pot last night?"

"Are you kidding? When did I have time to grind the coffee and set the timer?"

I laughed and pulled her closer. "Want some breakfast? Thanks to your shenanigans, we missed dinner last night."

"My shenanigans! More like yours. Yes, I'm starved and want one of your cowboy breakfasts."

"Home fries, the works?"

"Hold the steak."

I got busy, and soon we were wiping our mouths with our napkins. Jane said, "I've got an article with a deadline, so I'll be in my office for most of the morning."

"You mind if I take a drive? There's something I want to do."

"No problem. The keys are on the rack, the key with the miniature snaffle bit." She gave me a peck beside my mouth and disappeared into her office. This was a great time for a private phone call. I dialed the number on the scrap of paper.

"Perfect Circle Dressage," said the person on the other end.

"Is this Babs Longfellow?"

"It is. May I ask who's calling?"

"You don't know me. I'm Miles, and I'm from Montana, visiting a friend. Could I meet with you to discuss dressage?"

"What do you want to know? That's a big subject, Miles."

"I've gotten myself tangled up, trying to sort out something I have no business being involved in." Even to my ears it sounded lame.

"Having to do with riding dressage?"

"Megan Fisk and her horse's death. I have questions that I'd like to find answers for."

"Join the crowd. I have a half hour between lessons at ten o'clock. Can you be here then?"

"Can you tell me how to get there?"

"Sally! Come here a minute, will you, and give this woman directions. Thanks." She handed the phone off without even saying good-bye.

I made a note of the directions about thirty miles south of the Massachusetts border. This venture seemed really stupid, now that I'd committed to driving down there to talk with this trainer. What would I say? But then hadn't she said, "Join the crowd"? Babs must have doubts about Megan's death, too.

After I hung up the phone, I wandered outside. I had an hour to kill before I needed to get on the road. Scout saw me leave the house and jumped off the sofa, slipping past me as I shut the door. We walked out to the corrals. Strange that the boards made them paddocks. I had to think every time I called them that. Paddocks. I had a rush of longing for home and all that was familiar.

After a while, I called home to check in. My sweet brother answered the phone, "Miles residence. Norburt speaking."

"Nice job, Burt. Did Tess teach you that?" I smiled. He sounded like a butler in a grade B movie.

"Sis! It's you. Tess, it's my sister on the phone. She's calling me."

"Are you having fun? Tell me all you've been doing, and tell me about Alec. Is she close to foaling?"

"Alec is starting to bag up. We had pancakes and bacon for breakfast. Tess took me to the waterslide. Cousin Billy came, too. Then we had a picnic. We ate pasties and coleslaw. Tess brought little cups of pudding for dessert. Mine was butterscotch." Norburt's voice rose a couple of notches from the memory.

"That sounds like fun." I made a mental note to take him to the waterslide more often than once a year.

"It was. We are going to see the dinosaurs in Bozeman next."

"That's a neat museum. Life will be boring when I come home."

"Oh, no, sis. When are you coming back?"

"Ask Tess. She can show you on the calendar. How're the dogs? They being good?"

"Yes. They are both sleeping with me. Tess didn't want Skipper in the house, so we made a deal. I carried Skipper's bed and her water dish and her food and her toys over to my house. They think it's a camp-out."

"I miss you, Burt." And it was true.

I drove south in Jane's 4Runner over the Vermont line into Massachusetts. Rolling hills framed the valley formed by the Connecticut River, sliding in and out of view like a silver snake. The river had an uncanny, secretive, silent quality, deep with no ripples or rocks. The Missouri was like that, the only river in Montana that gave me the creeps.

Every so often, when I could get a chance, I loved throwing a dry fly on a rod over the quick Western rivers, bright and clear over rocks. Nothing like that flash of rainbow trout taking your cast fly, or even better, a cutthroat.

Maple trees covered the hills, a few early changers giving a hint of how riotous the forest would look in a week or two. In Vermont, fall colors were well ahead of Massachusetts. I got off the interstate at the small town Babs's assistant had mentioned, passed the general store, and followed a narrow paved road heading east. White board fences proclaimed this was horse country, and fancy country at that.

Horses wearing blankets on this warm fall day were scattered two or three to a turnout paddock. They picked at scant grass and tried to figure out how to scratch their itch trapped under the blankets.

I turned left into a driveway lined by these white fences, leading to a tidy arena and barn with flowers generously planted beside the entry doors and along the paddocks. Rich fall colors of zinnias and marigolds and their musky aroma met me at the door.

Babs had her feet on her desk, a gray lunch box open in front of her and half a sandwich in her hand when I walked into her office. She plunked her sandwich down on the wrapper and stuck out her hand. We shook while we sized each other up. I think it was generally favorable.

"I'm not even certain of what I want to ask you about. So I hope I don't waste your time."

"Hey. No problem. Sit down." Babs indicated a chair with a curled-up cat. The cat went onto my lap. Her warm fur felt good under my hands.

"It's a long and winding story, but basically I want to know what happened to Megan and her horse Threat Fear. Why she wanted to change trainers. All that."

"Megan." Babs's eyes got sad. "She was so gifted. And her horse."

"Did Megan say why she was switching trainers?"

After a few breaths worth of hesitation, she answered. "Now, you can't repeat this because it was never proven. It's terribly slanderous. She thought Georgia was drugging her horse to affect his performance, to dull him."

"Really? Did you tell this to the police?"

"No. I'll tell you, I honestly thought she might be fabricating this, perhaps to excuse Threat Fear's recent bad performance. And just for the record, this is a ruinous accusation to be passing around lightly. Didn't want to get in the middle of that one. I knew she and Georgia were having a…well, rough period recently."

"Breaking up?" I hit the nail on the head since she was trying to avoid hitting her thumb.

"Exactly," Babs said with relief. "So I took it with a grain of salt."

"What would you have done if it were true? About the drugs?"

"It was all moot, anyway. Or soon would've been. The horse would have either gone back to his former brilliance or been a candidate for an extended rest. In that case, she'd have to concentrate on Wyatt, and that one had lots of strings. In my opinion, Wyatt was not nearly in the same class as Threat Fury."

"Really? Georgia said she thought he was better than Fury. What's Wyatt's story?"

"The deal was that she would leave Wyatt and take Fury. I understand Georgia had her name on the bills of sale of both horses."

"Oh, I see what you mean about strings. If Georgia was even part owner, how could Megan move them without her permission?"

"That was one of the problems, getting it in writing," Babs said.

"Couldn't Megan buy back Georgia's half of the horse?"

"For what?"

"Wasn't Fury around fifteen hundred?"

"As a two-year-old, yes. Now he was worth seventy-five, eighty thousand. Georgia really had her over a barrel."

"So, why not just say, since there are two horses, Georgia take Wyatt and Megan take Fury, transfer papers and be shut of each other?"

"You just said the answer to that one. Any reasonable person would do that, but Georgia wouldn't throw away her handcuffs. If Georgia had formally objected, Megan couldn't have brought Fury here. I think Georgia didn't because she didn't want the gossip. They did have a written agreement that in the event of Megan's death, both horses' ownership went wholly to Georgia."

On the drive back to Putney, I thought this visit wasn't something I wanted to talk with Jane about yet. I wanted to let the information Babs had given me percolate. Besides, I wasn't sure it would help if I kept questioning events around the death of Megan. Jane's scruff was standing up already.

I'd picked up some fresh cod for dinner when I passed through Brattleboro. I put the fish in the fridge. Scout came bustling from the direction of Jane's office, gave one announcing bark at me, and then wiggled her greeting. I bent over to rub her hard little body covered with wirehair.

Jane called, "I'm putting the final touches to my article. It's due in the morning. Be out in a few minutes."

I dug around in the strange kitchen drawers looking for a potato peeler. Just about had everything set up when Scout began barking in earnest. The sound of a truck downshifting brought Jane into the living room. She pulled the curtain to one side to peer out. "Quiet, Scout. Here's my winter hay supply. Damn, I forgot it was coming today. Can you help?"

"You bet."

"I'll get you some gloves."

The guys had the truck backed up and the hay elevator in position by the time we walked to the barn. Figured they had done this before. Jane made brief introductions. The two, obviously father and son, remained silent, with a nod I might have missed if I had blinked. Jane and I went up the ladder to the loft. She stacked while I took them off the clanking, electric powered hay elevator and handed them up to her. We worked hard trying to keep up. During a lull, I said to Jane, "First time I've broken a sweat since I've been here."

She gave me a little sexy smile. "Good to keep you in shape."

The clanking began again, making us hustle to find room in the packed hayloft. Jane, on the top of the stack, shoved them close under the roof, and I tossed them up where she could get them. The end of the hay elevator jutted into the loft, the chain belt with hooks rumbling as the last bale traveled up from the wagon. I lifted it off and shouted our thanks to the farmer and his son.

"Take a break," I hollered to Jane. She crawled and slid down to me, and we sat in the open loft door to breathe air not filled with hay chaff. We watched the guys load the elevator and pull away.

Dust shimmered on the air, and I realized I felt sad and kind of distant from Jane. She seemed distracted all the time. It had to be Georgia. "You sure got yourself caught up in Georgia's life, didn't you?"

"God! Miles, can't you leave it?" Jane got up and climbed the stack. "Let's just finish this job, okay?"

"Sure thing." The bales weighed so little, I was tossing them around with one hand. With a little more power than was necessary, I might add. But I wasn't about to shut up. "I don't understand why you can't let Georgia weather this time out. People are fickle, but they also have short memories."

"You just don't understand, Miles."

"Explain to me what I don't."

"Megan did quite a lot to support that business, managed the lessons, and oversaw students to the shows. She was the one most people dealt with. Georgia doesn't have the people skills Megan had, except with the kids."

"I'll second that. So what obligation do you have to step into Megan's shoes?"

"Megan's death really threw Georgia for a loop. Knocked her off center. I just want to help her get back to functional."

We finished stacking the last bales. Jane sat on a bale and wiped her face with a handkerchief. "I thought you came out here to visit me. Instead, you've taken an unwarranted dislike to her, meddled in—"

"I don't like the way she simpers over you. And she's a smooth liar."

"Miles, you need to get your jealousy under control. What do I have to do?"

"Think up something."

We smiled. We kissed, our lips teasing at the corners of each other's mouths. When the warm breath from our noses mixed, I remembered doing that with horses when I was a kid. I believed that when you exchanged breath with a horse, you understood each other; you were sisters. Of course, there were a lot of kids with bitten noses. Dust motes floated on the sunshine flooding in through the open hayloft door. The air sparkled like fairy dust.

I looked at Jane, who had climbed back up the stack, and instead of tossing the last bale, I broke it open. "Come on. Get in the truck."

She laughed as she slid down to the soft hay. "I'd forgotten your Western foreplay. So touching in its simplicity."

I liked the way she looked as she lay before me, dusty, sweaty, real. I nestled in next to her, drawing in her scent, the fluffy cloud of her hair brushing my cheeks. Jane grabbed my forearms, one in each hand and squeezed. "What a turn-on your arms are, so strong. I can make out each muscle."

"Comes from all that bale tossing. The real thing bales, eighty to ninety pounds, not these thirty-pound snacks."

Jane laughed, too. "I have to admit when I came back home, they did seem tiny."

I pulled her to me close and held her. The earthy aroma of hay and Jane's scent filled my senses. Our lips touching in that first taste of her, salty with a hint of coffee and alfalfa, gathered all my senses. The last light of day brought Scout's whine up to the hayloft. We laughed and stood, brushing the alfalfa leaves from each other's shoulders.

Chapter Eight

The early morning breeze lifted the curtains in Jane's bedroom, and I felt her body curled along mine, her breath brushing my shoulder in soft puffs. I was fully awake, tingling in those places Jane could so easily reach. I lay there for a few minutes idly wondering what had awakened me, then settled my head against the down pillow, enjoying the closeness of Jane. Her scent. I must be in love; even her breath smelled sweet.

The birds were raucous, becoming louder by the minute. I had to pee. That was it. Hard to relax and enjoy lying in bed when you must get to the bathroom. Pronto. I grabbed my jeans and a T-shirt on my way there. Relieved, I padded out to the kitchen. In the middle of filling the kettle, I realized it was too early for coffee and all the racket that went with making it. I'd just go outside. My tennis shoes were beside the door, and so was Scout.

The air felt crisp with dew on the blades of grass. Everything here in Vermont was so green, you could smell it growing. Lushness to the point of rankness, like I should approach the growth with a machete strapped to my hip. Birds flitted and danced in the bushes, alarmed. Perhaps they thought I looked suspicious standing there unmoving when I should be on my way somewhere else. The barn drew me toward it like a magnet. Mare and pony saw me and gave breakfast calls. I'd feed them, mostly to quiet them so Jane could sleep. A few barn swallows flew out as I entered, catching my attention to admire their swoops and dives. Dust motes flickered bright on the air. The barn aroma stopped me in my tracks: hay and straw, leather, horse breath.

A foolish grin grew on my face as I drew in large, deep breaths. The things that make us happy. I took the hayfork and tossed a few flakes of hay into the wall feeder in the run-in, then just leaned on the fork and listened to those lovely sounds of horses eating.

Jane found me, brushing Moon Glow while she ate her hay. "There you are! Coffee's made. Getting your horse fix?"

I grinned at her. "Guess so."

She held out her hand for me to take. "Let's have coffee. Later, shall we go for a ride?"

I remembered the last one. Must have frowned.

"Just the two of us," Jane said. "And no Cat. I'll call Victoria and see if we can borrow Night."

"That would be swell." The desire to be on the back of a good horse came in a rush. Maybe this was what they called "pleasure riding." Just because it was fun and not a lick of work to do, salt to pack, cows to move, fences to check.

While Jane was on the phone, I got out a skillet and cracked four eggs into some butter. Strawberries got a quick shower, then into a bowl. Future toast down the slots. Breakfast was nearly ready by the time she returned with a smile on her face. "Vic has all day meetings and is happy we'll take her horse out of the barn."

"Good." I slapped the eggs and toast on plates and sat down.

"You expect me to eat all this?" Jane eyed the two frieds and toast on her plate.

"Well, yes. I didn't give you any steak or pie."

"I should hope not!"

I noticed she sat down and cleaned her plate, in spite of the largesse.

Funny. I surprised myself by feeling a rising anticipation of the horse between my legs. I never much thought about riding at home. I just went out, saddled up who I was going to ride that day, and rode out to do the job that was needed. However, I couldn't deny to myself that lift of spirits horses brought to me, the feeling of my heart wide open. We each filled a go cup with coffee and drove north with the car windows rolled down.

Georgia's barn was surprisingly quiet. The swallows were busy, though, swooping and twittering. Georgia wasn't around, I happily noted. We saddled Dusty and Night, and then Jane let Scout out of the car and mounted up. Scout danced around in ecstasy.

"Poor thing. She doesn't get as many rides with Dusty not home."

"Skippy's the same, always ready." I wished my sweet border collier were here now.

"I guess to them it's the ultimate walk."

"So, why don't you bring Dusty home? I don't get the point of keeping him forty miles from where you live."

"There are such advantages to keeping him here for the summer months. I can ride with Vic. Lots of riding clinics are held within a short distance. Georgia can school me out of my sloppy habits."

"You're a way better rider than her. She rides like a poker is up—"

"Miles! I do believe you're jealous. Let's gallop." Jane's gelding made a smooth transition into a canter. All very polite and controlled.

I whooped, gave Night some rein, and we surged past her at a full-out gallop. Boy, that mare could cover some ground. I heard a shriek behind me, and Dusty picked up the pace. I looked over my shoulder, saw the smile on Jane's face, and relaxed into the full-stride run. We were approaching a sharp curve, so I sat up deep and set my hand. Night easily slowed to a canter. Jane came up beside me, the horses snorting, jumping in energy-loaded canter-leaps.

We both laughed. "Oh, God, that was fun. But so bad for training."

"They loved it as much as you did. Horses aren't supposed to have any fun? Not one of us animals can be controlled all the time and stay healthy."

She gave me a funny look. "You're right. I don't suppose they can."

I reached across the space and touched her arm. "Horses are an extension of myself. Only when I'm on one am I wholly who I am. Perhaps I'm a centaur."

Jane smiled at me. "That may be where the idea came from."

"There's that part of you that wants to be more of a wild creature, a very attractive aspect of you. For me. Others will want to tame it." I knew all remnants of my smile had left my face, even my eyes.

Jane nodded. "People have."

"Don't let them."

Chapter Nine

"Want to go out tonight?" Vic's blue eyes held a devilish gleam.

"Where?" Jane asked, pulling one of the patio chairs out with her foot. "Have a seat. And a cup of java."

Victoria plunked down and reached for the coffeepot. When she'd filled her carry cup, she said to me with one raised eyebrow, "Just getting up? I thought you ranchers are early risers."

"I did wake up early." I could feel the skin around my eyes crinkling.

A contented humming purr came from Jane. She held her coffee cup just under her nose so the warmth of the coffee could rise to meet her. I smiled at her.

"You two are like old dogs, never going far from the hearth." Victoria got a kick out of us.

I grinned sheepishly. "You're not far wrong. It's the bed, though, not the hearth." I held up my wrist to see the time. One o'clock. By God, I'd have some major time adjustments to do when I got home. And sloth adjustments.

"What's on your devious mind?" Jane prodded.

"Brattleboro's very own gay bar. Let's go dancing."

Here was a straight woman wanting to go to a gay bar to

dance? I'm liberal and all, but this was a new one on me. "Will Michael be joining us?"

"He hates to dance. And those disco lights flashing and turning make him sick to his stomach. No, just a girls' night out. Want to?"

Jane lowered her eyes at me, like inviting me to go play. "Sure," we both said at once.

"We could go out to dinner first at that swank restaurant with a view over the river."

"You mean that Thai one? That is good," Jane said in agreement.

"Thai food. I haven't had anything exotic other than Mexican since I hauled some horses to Calgary one time. Years ago. That's the closest place with international food outside of Seattle. Only seven hours' drive away," I added with irony.

"Then now's the time to take advantage. Terrific. I'll go home, shower, and put on the dog. Shall I meet you back here at five?"

"Let's do it," Jane said. "I'll make reservations for six."

"Wait! I don't have much in the way of fancy clothes." I knew these gals were going to be shining, and I didn't want to look too dull next to them.

Victoria eyed me up and down. "Wear your cowgirl boots. Michael and you are about the same size. What, thirty-four long? And he has a robin's egg blue silk shirt that would look dynamite. And a vest. Should about do it." She snapped the cap on her coffee mug and stood. "I better get back here at four thirty so we can dress you."

Back in my youth, in high school, I'd missed all this "girl" stuff. I was a blank slate in these two women's hands. I presented myself, showered, with clean fingernails and underwear, and they did the rest.

The pants fit like they'd been tailored. Black with tiny

pleats at the hipbones, they hung well, if I do say so myself. My black city boots were studly. The blue shirt looked good, too. Long sleeved with discreet cuff links offered up by Jane. I wore a matte black vest with thin dark red stripes in the front panel over the shirt. Somehow, though, it didn't quite come together.

Jane sat in a soft corduroy-covered chair and painted her nails. Scout lay curled up at her feet. In between concentration on the accuracy of the paint, she made comments. "The outfit needs something. Try some of the silk scarves from my dresser. Top right drawer." She waved one hand slowly, fingers spread like a seal flipper.

"That's it!" said Victoria, diving for the dresser. She scooped up a handful of brightly colored scarves and spread them on the bed. She picked out a large one with different bright blues all over in a pattern, folded it in a triangle, and tied it around my neck in the style of the 1920s film cowgirls.

I untied it, handed it back to Vic, then reached to the bed and picked up a solid red, small scarf, made it into a triangle, then spun it into a thin rope and tied that around my neck under the collar. With a lean smile, I nodded at the blue scarf in Victoria's hand. "That's a girl scarf."

"Ooh, how butch," Vic said.

"That's my honey," Jane said, waving the other hand like she was a parade queen. The bright paint was eye catching, like little neon signs at the tips of her fingers.

"We better get going," Vic advised. "It's five thirty now."

Jane pulled on her black silk slacks and a lovely black silk tunic, covered with blazing dragons in embroidery thread.

We came together, arm in arm in front of the full-length mirror, swaying sideways to get the full picture, and we were quite a bunch. Vic came close to looking as butch as I did in her vest, crisp white shirt, and tan slacks with a turned-up cuff.

At the door, I grabbed my Stetson, the usual dress-up thing to do. Victoria touched my arm. "No. Don't ruin your hair. We spent so long on it. And this isn't that sort of bar."

"What do you mean?"

Jane explained, "There are bars where all the guys wear cowboy hats and high-heeled boots even if they've never been outside city limits. I don't think you want to send the message they're striving for."

I wondered, but the conversation had gone as far as I wanted.

Victoria parked the car on Western Avenue, a street lined with big old houses set back from the road and tall trees that had been planted along the street when the boards to build the houses were still seeping sap. We walked, laughing and talking, down the steep hill toward the center of town and the wide Connecticut River.

Dinner was great, a real kick to the taste buds. We watched the light change on the river, shadows deepening, turning the water from silver-blue to secretive purple. One lone canoe paddled downriver, returning with a couple from their day out. Over coffee and a single malt scotch, a teenaged Lagavulin with just the right amount of smokiness, we hoped we hadn't burdened ourselves with too much food. Dessert had been discussed and rejected in the interest of being lighter on our feet dancing.

The club wasn't far from the restaurant, so we walked. We went a little out of our way to let dinner settle and to watch the evening light play on the Connecticut River. A few ducks, looking panicky in their quick-winged way, flew up river. Scraps of sound flew back to us, quacks on an off key.

"Enough of nature. Let's go dancing," Vic said.

"My, you are eager," Jane said with a smile.

I asked Vic, "Don't you wonder if people will assume you're lesbian?"

"Probably about as much as you worry they'll think you're straight."

Damn, I could see why Jane loved this woman.

The bar was an enormous, sunken room with two tiers of seating clustered around small tables. To one side a separate dance floor and hot, loud dance music called to us. It didn't take long for Victoria to have more dance offers than she could handle.

She said, sitting down for a breather and waving away another butch with a smile, "I should have brought a dance card."

"You're a great dancer," I observed. "You gals are lucky to have this place. We have our choice of a seedy little bar in Billings and the Elks club in Missoula, which is supposed to be gay-friendly. Both are unbelievably depressing."

A slow tune came on, and I grabbed my girl's hand. Lightly holding each other, we moved around the floor, our bodies caressing the small space between us.

Chapter Ten

W hat happened to the horse?" The question had just popped into my head. Jane and I were raking leaves into a pile in the middle of her driveway. Absently, I struck a small wooden match against the box's grit to light a wad of paper beneath the pile. The smoke smelled sweet. I looked at Jane, waiting for an answer.

"What horse?"

"Threat Fury?" When I said the horse's name, something nagging my brain came thundering to the forefront. It was Megan's private dare to Georgia and the horse show world to name her horse after a well-known lesbian musician.

I hit my forehead and shook my head. We both got the name's significance at the same time. "Do you think we would have ever figured it out if we hadn't learned about their being lovers?" I asked Jane. "I wonder if Georgia knew Megan had named her horse after Tret Fure."

"I'll ask her."

"Call her. Ask her, too, about what happened to the horse. Was it buried on the farm? Or was the body removed? I'll watch the fire." I was flaming with curiosity as I jabbed the smoking leaves with my rake to show her how attentive I could be.

Jane was at the back door when I thought to yell, "Ask her about the dead horse first. She might be too flipped about Megan's private joke."

Jane frowned and opened the screen door.

What I wouldn't give to be the proverbial fly on the wall up at Georgia's facility. Nothing like a homophobic, smug gal being privately outed to other queers by association and not even knowing it. I would lay good odds on this being a news flash, that Megan had played with the name of a well-known and out lesbian. Jane was a much nicer person than I was and would not have half the glee I felt just anticipating the look on Georgia's face.

I leaned on the rake looking at the Green Mountains, Vermont's spine. They must have been named in the spring or summer because now they were a mix of orange and red, with patches of dark green.

About fifteen minutes later, a somber Jane returned. "She was utterly furious. Hadn't a clue and said she'd have killed her if she'd known. Gave me the shivers."

"Had no idea, did she?" My smile was about to engulf my whole face. What's called a shit-eating grin.

"You're enjoying this way too much," Jane said, very serious and Quakerly. Then a sliver of a smile crept into her eyes. The laugh burst out with lots of spit when it came.

"Megan's private rebellion."

Jane nodded in agreement. "Georgia can be very controlling."

"Why are you friends with her, Jane? So far I haven't seen much to like." I hadn't often seen Jane Scott act evasive. She was now. Flat out changed the subject.

"The dead horse disposal people came and hauled him away."

"Oh?" I studied her, but she busied herself raking and wouldn't make eye contact. "Mink farm? Who picks up dead horses around here?"

Jane looked up at me. "It would have to be a mink farm or a rendering plant."

"Well? Which one?" I waited, leaning on my rake.

"I don't know, she didn't say. There can't be many firms offering that service in New England."

"Could be someone offers both services. Have to admit, Jane, none of this adds up. Do you mind if we find out? Snoop a little?"

"I can look it up." Jane again headed for the house.

This time when I shouted after her, I asked her to bring me a pop. It didn't take her long to return with a nice cold can of Mountain Dew. One brand I'm not familiar with. Wasn't bad either.

"The only place in Vermont is a two-hour drive north. They pick up all dead animals. There's one in Maine, but that place is an eight-hour drive. What's shifting around in your mind, anyway?"

"Curiosity, mostly. I wonder what they did with him if he was given a lethal injection. I understood the only thing you could do is bury them or render them for fertilizer."

"Oh! Depressing to think of that gorgeous horse feeding plants. Or mink, for that matter. Want to go, or call?" Jane said.

A soft breeze wiggled her curls, and the freckles over her nose stood out like the spots on the rump of an Appaloosa horse. She looked so cute I had a rush to pick her up and carry her into the house.

She must have read it in my eyes, for she smiled and said, "We've already done that this morning. There are only two choices before you. Drive. Call."

"Darn." I drawled out the word for more effect. "Let's drive, it'll be fun to see more of the state. And when you call the offices, you never get the skinny. You know, the person who actually picked up the horse."

Jane got the hose and sprayed out the fire.

"Scout wants to come with us," I observed.

Scout stood eagerly wagging her erect tail, looking back and forth at us. She knew we were discussing her. Jane smiled at her. "Come on, little dog." Scout shot toward Jane's car. I opened the back door, and she leaped onto the back and curled up in her bed, which always lived there.

The smell of the place was rank. The only one who could stand it was Scout, who stood with her feet on the window edge, twitching her black nose. Between the piled-up mink shit under the cages and the cut-up, waiting-to-be-devoured, fly-covered carcasses of various species of animals, it wasn't pretty. Maybe the phone would have been the way to go after all. We found the owner.

"Do you remember picking up a dead horse at North Winds Farm a little south of Woodstock? It was just over two months ago. This was a large sorrel horse. Destroyed by a lethal shot," Jane said.

"Lead or drug?" His eyes were playful.

"Injection," I put in. "Might have been some talk about this horse. He was worth a bundle."

"No. I wouldn't have picked up a horse destroyed by drugs. Can't feed 'em out, you know? All the fertilizer horses go to my cousin, and he charges to pick 'em up."

Jane grabbed my arm at the elbow, "Let's not bother him

any more." She held her nostrils closed, so she sounded like "Ledz nod buddor em eddy moo."

I wanted to make sure. "The farm owner gave us your name."

Jane narrowed her eyes at me and turned her head a little to one side. He looked blank and screwed his lips up, pursing them to help the thought process.

"Nice farm with a big barn and four-bar split-rail fence either side of the driveway. Roomy solid oak stalls. Might have been hard to fish him out of the stall. The woman you dealt with, her name is Georgia and the guy works for her is Arthur."

Finally, I fed him enough reminders that the memories clicked in. "You're wrong there. No wonder I couldn't place the animal. We're rugged careful about drug residues for our little minks. That horse didn't have a lethal injection. He was accidentally electrocuted."

"No. This horse had a—" I stopped myself. "Who told you the horse died that way?"

"I remember, 'cause the horse's owner, Mary or something, no Morgan, my sister's name, killed herself, too. That farm owner said something about she was clipping the horse and the clippers fell into a bucket of water. Something like that. So that's why I took the animal to feed my minkies with."

Jane and I faced each other. I clamped my jaw tight to keep it from slacking.

"Did you read about it in the papers?" Jane asked.

While he ranged back in his memory, I watched mesmerized by a drip forming at the end of his nose. He wiped it off with one knuckle of his right hand. Slowly, after scanning all the memory banks, he shook his head. "Can't say I did. Get the St. Johnsbury paper once in a while. Jeezem Crow, not never much news in it. Just stuff about Iraq or Iran. Never can keep 'em straight. I don't care what them little countries do. The high school basketball, now that's news. We near beat Burlington last week."

CHAPTER ELEVEN

He is mistaken. Got two different stops mixed up, that's all. That horse was rendered for fertilizer. Only thing you can do with a horse that's had drugs." Georgia opened a door marked *Feed Room* to shout inside, "Arthur, mind you check each bag for mold when you pour them in the bins."

A dark mumbling issued from the room.

We had stopped at North Winds Farms on our way south. With this explanation, I felt more than saw Jane's body soften. And I had to admit that I'd thought this, too. After a day picking up horse corpses, the details must get fuzzy. But he was so explicit about the "girl, Morgan" who died with her horse. At that moment, Georgia turned on me, and I had a glimpse of what Arthur went through every day.

"What were you doing checking up on me, anyway?" Her blue eyes were like carbide boring bits.

Although this was directed at me, I let Jane respond. I figured it would be good for her to meet that corner of Georgia that was not so nice.

Stepping closer to me, Jane said, "I wanted to show Miles more of the state. We weren't checking up on you, but we were curious."

Georgia responded with a tight smile of disbelief and

arms folded across her chest, and it must have wilted Jane's explanation.

I decided to put in my nickel's worth. "I was curious about what the mink would eat. If they fed them meat from animals destroyed with some lethal substance. We stopped for my own education."

"Oh? And why would you need to know?" She jabbed at me with icicle words.

I took my cap off and slapped it on my leg. I did this mostly to hide my smile. I knew we'd hooked her. She was way too curious about my motives.

"I've got an elderly horse it's time I thought about putting down before winter. I don't think I could put a gun to this old friend's head. Thought of calling a vet to come out with drugs. On the other hand, I don't want to poison any predators who might eat from the body. It's too rocky at my ranch to bury them deep. So, Georgia, I wanted to know how the mink handle the drugs. Or maybe there's a new one. But they said this horse wasn't drugged, he was electrocuted."

I could see the woman shifting around, eyes and feet in a dance. "He's wrong. That's all there is to it." The feet took over. "I'm busy. My Pony Club kids are due any minute. Call me later, Jane."

The unspoken desire to never hear from me again in her lifetime was clear.

I sat staring through the 4Runner's windshield as we drove south to Putney. Jane asked me, "Why are you prodding her? It's really rude. The police don't think she's involved in Megan's death, yet you don't seem to be able to accept that."

"Prodding her? My God, Jane, she's totally homophobic. There are some people who make the hair rise on the back of my neck. She's one of them. I'm sorry she's your friend. I can't figure it, based on what I know of you."

"I hope that at some point she may grow to accept herself, if not love herself."

"An admirable, but unlikely change. She's nervous about something. Maybe it's related to Megan or her horse's death and maybe not." I scratched my head to get it to work better and wondered why Jane was so blind to Georgia's faults. I figured it was time to head straight into Jane's loyalty. "Yesterday I talked with the trainer where Megan planned on moving her horse. Babs Longfellow."

Jane flicked her glance at me. "I know her. She's very respected."

"She said Megan thought Georgia had been doing something to dim the brilliance of Fury. Some kind of drug."

"That's one hell of an accusation. She's treading on thin ice to pass that bit of dirt around."

"Babs was very careful about this and wasn't out to spread dirt. She was trying very tactfully to let me know Megan's reason for bringing her horse to her farm. Okay, Jane. Come clean with me. What are you doing with all this loyalty to Georgia? You're not seeing clearly."

Jane pursed her lips, flashing me a side look. She downshifted the 4Runner at a turn, concentrating on her driving. I knew she was doing some heavy thinking about what I'd said, so I gave her some time to respond. Finally she did, a touch of anger in her voice. I'd call it belligerence except that I love her.

"I never dreamed that you'd come here at this time, or involve yourself so much in this affair."

"It wasn't a frivolous decision, Jane. The plane fare took a big chunk out of my savings. I had to find out about my competition."

"There's nothing I can do to prevent you from feeling

competitive, if you choose. But it is irrelevant. I have history with her."

We were getting to the nitty gritty now, and I knew we had to push whatever this was out into the open. "Okay, so tell me what your 'history' is?" And then to my surprise, I saw Jane blush. "You didn't have an affair with her at summer camp, did you?" I laughed out loud.

"No."

"A lot of girls have their first love at camp, you know. You wouldn't be the Lone Ranger."

"I said no."

"Okay, Jane. I'm done messing around. Tell me the hold she has on you."

We pulled into her driveway, and I watched as she turned the key. The engine died, but she kept sitting there, staring out through the windshield. Scout gave a soft whine.

After a few moments, she said, "I've never told anyone about this. I'm the one responsible for outing her to her parents. Even Georgia doesn't know this." She turned and aimed her gaze at me. "And I don't want you to tell her."

"Oh? How did this happen?"

"I was a counselor at a Pony Club summer camp. You have to remember I was only eighteen. Georgia was sixteen at the time and totally smitten with a B level Pony Clubber named Della who had come with her family from Peru. Della was tall with totally gorgeous bone structure. All the girls had crushes on her. We thought of her as the Incan Queen of the Andes.

"We lost out, though. Della must have been attracted to Georgia's aloof Anglo looks. Georgia's cabin was the one I was responsible for. She started sneaking out after she thought the rest of us were asleep, and they'd spend the whole night out under the stars. I'd lie there and pray for rain. They'd pass little notes and look longingly at each other. Everybody noticed."

"This happens all the time. What was the big deal?"

"I took it upon myself to write Georgia's parents and enclose a love letter she'd sent to Della. I found it under Della's pillow. I told them she had a 'special friendship,' and I thought she needed to see a therapist. Claimed this sort of behavior was unacceptable and disturbed the other campers."

"Jane. What a shitty thing to do. What got into you?"

Here, not only did she blush a deeper red, she couldn't meet my eyes. "Although I'd convinced myself I was shocked by their depravity, the real truth was, I wanted Della with a vengeance." Jane looked up at me and held my gaze with a stark honesty.

I shook my head slowly and smiled. Not many people could admit to something like that. And most of us have a knot in our rope.

"I've never told a soul. Oh, of course in the shallow front of my brain, I had convinced myself that she must be stopped from perversion. But deep inside, I knew I wanted to do some perversion with Della. I came out shortly after this happened."

At last this murky little secret was in the light. "You didn't make Georgia what she is today, Jane."

"If I'd had any idea how horribly her parents would behave, I never would have told them. They called, and I answered the phone in the camp office. I was the one who had to tell Georgia that her parents would arrive the following day to pick her up. Later Georgia sat on my bunk and cried. So many times that long night I almost told her that her pain was because of me. The next morning they came for her, and I didn't see her again until recently."

"Time to put it to rest, my dear. She's a big girl and can

stand on her own." Jane stared out the windshield, her face overlain with pain and horror. She was silent for so long I got worried. "What is it?"

"One evening, after a lesson I'd given an adult beginner, we went to dinner together. We had wine with dinner, then sat out on the patio and drank margaritas. I'm sure what she told me had more to do with the tequila than our friendship." Jane looked at me, her gaze laced with sadness. "I can't tell you what she said, because I swore secrecy. You know, the 'stick a needle in your eye' kind."

"So, why are you telling me about a conversation you can't tell me about?"

"All I can tell you is that when she got back home after the summer camp experience, something awful happened to her. I have more empathy for her as a result."

Chapter Twelve

The *Worchester Telegram and Gazette* crackled as Jane removed it from the plain brown envelope. No return address. Someone had sent her the local page, underlining the headline in red Magic Marker.

"What's this?" Jane shook the paper. No personal note fell out. "Who sent it?"

I examined the manila envelope. "The postmark date is smeared."

We huddled close, scanning the story from a paper printed three weeks ago.

Sensational journalism. A blowup color photograph of the head and forelegs of Megan's horse, dead in his stall, took up most of the front page. Megan's hand showed in the frame. Her fingers were like a dead spider lying on its back. Crossing her palm was an empty twenty-cc syringe with the plunger pushed in all the way.

While the lead news was about the dead rider who had been headed for the Olympics, there was a local angle. This ugly death occurred at a stable run by a local woman, gone away and made good. It was really about Georgia. The story revealed Georgia's lowly beginnings. Somehow the paper had dug up information on Georgia's youthful shoplifting charges and other minor theft. She'd done community service restitution for malicious mischief.

The family's lives were turned around when Georgia's mother invented the Rainstorm Hula Loop. Leaving Worcester behind, they moved as millionaires to a farm in Vermont and put the daughter in Pony Club.

"What a contrast. Rags to riches. Do you have any idea when they moved to Vermont?"

"I'd guess the big change happened when she was anywhere between twelve and fifteen. That's a hard age for things to alter so radically."

"Yeah, to go from one of the many poor kids on the block to being able to have anything you wanted. No wonder she's so nervous about protecting her socially acceptable personage."

"I remember she always tried so hard to fit in. Her parents came to visit her on Parents Day, and she'd rush to the car and never introduce them. She came back from the obligatory lunch in town, loaded with candy bars. She doled them out on a 'best friend' basis. But I don't recall her having any real friends."

"She must have been a lonely kid."

Jane picked up the envelope and looked it over. "I wonder who sent this. And why?"

I didn't answer because something about the photo bothered me. Jane had shown me photos of Megan riding Threat Fury in the dressage ring and over a jumping course. I hadn't remembered any partial white on the feet, but here in the picture the left front leg had a white spot the size of a walnut immediately above the hoof wall. And the star on his forehead had little points and roaning hair, which made it not neat and trim.

"I wonder where the paper got this picture," I said, looking at Jane. "From the sheriff's office? What's the procedure?"

Jane furrowed her eyebrows and looked back at me. "I don't get what you're asking."

"Could they have set up this picture for the newspaper? Faked it? Do presses ever do that?"

She reached over and took the page from me. "What are you concerned about? It is sensational to print it. But I expect it sells—"

"No. Jane. This dead horse isn't Threat Fury. In the snapshots you showed me, Megan was riding a horse with no white, except a small tidy star on his forehead."

"How can you be so sure?"

"I'm not sure," I said as soothingly as I could muster. "But I'd lay odds that this dead horse is Wyatt, and the horse standing in the barn at Georgia's is Threat Fury."

"My God! That's fantastic!" Jane stared at me, mouth slightly ajar, and her eyes wide. "That would mean that Georgia knows, is somehow involved. Miles, that is too much. You've gone too far."

"I want to see those pictures again."

"You can't. They're in Georgia's office, and she's away at an event." Jane's eyes weren't focused on me.

"Can I borrow your car?"

Jane's voice rose a few notches in volume. "Why are you doing all this? What are you planning? Break into her office or something? Can't you leave her alone? Can't you get it through your head, Miles, that she's done nothing? You're fabricating an involvement that can't possibly exist. Arthur would know that the horses were switched. There's no way—"

"Who do you think sent this? Arthur *does* know, and he's trying to make us figure it out." I shook the newspaper. "Are you that much like her, Jane? Do you have to be so blind? She's mixed up in something, and I want to find out."

Jane turned her back on me and walked out of the room.

"What a mess! Go! Try to dig up your dirt, but keep me out of it. The keys are hanging to the left of the door."

I thought about us all the way to North Winds Farm. My guts felt like broken glass had gotten inside. When I walked down the dark aisle toward the office, with sounds of munching hay on both sides of me, I tried to visualize the door unlocked.

It wasn't. So much for creative visualization.

Arthur rounded the corner of the aisle, pushing the grain cart. He came to a sudden halt when he saw me. I had the strangest impression that he was about to bolt, but he stood riveted to the ground with a grain scoop in his hand. The next horses in line grew impatient. Sharp demanding neighs rang out, and horses circled their stalls.

I approached him, drawing the newspaper clipping out of my pocket. He would know the horse. The person who picked out feet and brushed silky legs could identify an animal better than any photograph.

"Arthur," I began.

"I didn't send Ms. Scott that."

"No. Of course not. I wanted to show you this picture." I unfolded it. "What horse is this?"

"It says Threat Fury." Arthur was playing with me.

"But it's not, is it?" His sly smile was the answer. "Who is it then? I'm sure you know every hair of every horse at North Winds."

He glowed with the pleasure of being acknowledged, then he pinched his eyes and twitched his lips. "You'll find Fury in another horse's stall."

"Wyatt. They were switched. Wyatt was the murdered horse."

He scrunched up his face as he fought back tears. "Had a little bit of white on one heel."

"Who do you think switched them, Arthur?"

"Wouldn't know about that," he murmured. He pushed the cart along, and I had to quickly step aside.

I watched him lumbering down the aisle, stopping every pair of stalls to measure out each horse's ration. The horses called to the familiar figure, some shrilly, others with soft rumbles. He had loved Wyatt, and I imagined he had few opportunities to feel love.

I wondered about the likelihood of confirming Fury's identity. Sorting through the rules of different breed registries was a paper jungle to me. DNA records were on file for breeding stock of most purebred organizations, but Threat Fury was a gelding, so he might not have a DNA record. Although his father was a Danish Warmblood, his mother was a cross of thoroughbred and draft horse. I think I remembered Jane saying he was registered as a part blood with the Warmblood Society. His sire's blood type would be on record. Perhaps DNA would prove the stallion had sired the horse everyone in this barn called Wyatt. I decided to pull a bit of mane by the roots from the horse I thought was Threat Fury.

What the heck, I'd send it in for a match. What else was I doing with my summer vacation? Doing my best to alienate the woman I loved, for one thing. I couldn't bring it to a halt, though. It seemed like one thing led to the next, and I kept having more questions. It was all too slick. I was becoming convinced that Georgia had murdered Megan and had set the whole thing up. She hadn't been able to destroy the better of the two horses, though. A little part of me wondered if the reason she had selected Wyatt as a backup was because they were so close in appearance. How many people would notice a one-inch circle of white on a foot, most often covered by bedding or grass? And a star was a star on a horse's forehead to most people. But I'd dated a brand inspector for a while.

She taught me more about noticing those little marks than I'd ever been aware of before.

On the way to Wyatt/Fury's stall, I swung by the wash rack and got a plastic bag from the wall cabinet. While in the stall with the horse, I checked for any white on his legs. I cleared the wood shavings away from each hoof so I could see the coronet band. Nothing. He had a small, clean-edged white star on his forehead.

It was a simple matter to pull some of the horse's mane. My brand inspector sweetheart had shown me how to do it; the little sack at the root of the hairs had to be included. That gal was proving very valuable in retrospect. I carefully rolled the sample in the bag.

Shutting his stall door I heard, "Where's Jane?" Mumble, mumble. "Well, I see her car out there."

My mind flipped around like a caged animal, desperately coming up with the silliest ideas: hiding in a stall, running outside and concealing myself in the bushes until Georgia left. Things like that.

A strange inability to move had frozen me to the ground when Georgia rounded the end of the aisle leading a blanketed and leg-wrapped white horse. She came to a halt. Wordlessly, we stared at each other for an endless moment while I slipped the small bag into my back pocket.

She asked that pompous question people ask when they want to say *What the hell are you doing here?*: "Can I help you?"

The explanation for my invasion of her barn popped into my head. "Jane thought she'd left her gloves."

"Oh?" Georgia arched her eyebrows. "I don't recall she wore any the last time she was here."

"Must have left them in the grocery store. How did Naomi do?" I'd recognized her gelding as the one Georgia led.

"Ms. Bly took first place. I would like you to call before you come to this facility." Her smile was thin, with enough warmth to glaze the ice.

"Why, I'll keep that in mind." I returned my best insincere smile, showing a lot of teeth.

We had no illusions or pretenses. We detested each other. How much of it was jealousy, I couldn't say.

"Going home to Wyoming soon?" she asked.

"You bet."

Outside the Putney General store, I'd picked up an express envelope from the FedEx stand. Jane was working in the garden when I returned.

"What have you been up to?"

I held up the plastic bag. "Took a little hair sample. Arthur admitted the horse in the stall is Threat Fury, so I thought it would be interesting to confirm that."

"Interesting?" Jane said dryly. "You know what this means, don't you?"

"The whole death is a setup. Arthur knows and Georgia must, too."

"Why have you taken this on, Miles?"

"Don't know. Maybe it's some mean part of me trying to drive a wedge between you and Georgia. Or maybe the whole thing seems fishy, and I can't let it go." I asked her if she'd find the North American Danish Warmblood Registry's address on her computer. When she did, I block lettered it onto the label.

Inside the envelope I placed the hair and a cover letter asking them to check the sample against Threat Fury's sire's DNA. Wyatt's wasn't on record anywhere because he was a homegrown warmblood, a Belgian draft horse and thoroughbred cross mother and a thoroughbred father. I asked the registry to respond to Jane's email address, as well as hard copy proof. Told them if they sent a phone number, I'd call with a credit card number for them to charge for their services.

"This way we'll know," I said to Jane.

"You'll know. But will it stop all this foolishness?"

I looked at her long and hard, feeling a soft warmth for her. Her loyalty was working overtime for Georgia, that was all. "Arthur told me they'd been switched. Who would know better than he?"

Jane sat silently, but I could see her mind wasn't closed. The wheels behind her eyes were turning. She dropped her head into her open hands.

I took both her hands in mine and said, "There's something going on here—look at me, Jane—and it's not on the level. Maybe Megan switched them hoping to kill Wyatt and collect on Fury. Who knows? It may have nothing to do with Georgia. But it makes you wonder why she's said nothing. She must know the horse in Wyatt's stall is Fury."

Jane withdrew her hands from mine and leaned back. "Since you seem bent on looking for a murderer for Megan, why not look at Arthur?"

I snorted at the absurdity of it. As soon as I'd made my burst of sound, I knew it was a mistake. Jane jumped to her feet and stormed out the door to the garden. She pulled her spading fork out of the dirt.

"Damn it! Why are you so against her? Arthur could have come across Megan in the act of killing her horse and killed her in a rage."

"With a horseshoe he picked up beside the stall door?" I never would have guessed brindle brown eyes could be so chilly. "You're right Jane, it's a stretch. What I've learned, though, is that it is beyond belief that Megan would kill either one of her horses."

I leaned against the stone wall and said, "If this is Threat

Fury disguised as Wyatt, Georgia is a player in this murder. I don't know what she's done or why, but I promise you, honey, I'm going to find out."

"Miles, I'm disturbed by all this. What has she done that makes you go for her throat? Is it chemistry? You seem so unrelenting. You take the word of a nasty, sour old man who hates Georgia and blow it up out of all proportion. Maybe he switched them."

I stared at the woman I loved with my guts in agony, my heart in distress, and my mind churning. "Georgia is after you because you're rich. Plain and simple."

"Oh, don't be silly."

"Having money is such a casual thing for you, it makes you blind to other people's motivation."

"You mean like kids being best friends with me because I have more candy?"

"Exactly. I was the kid who was drawn to kids like you. I never had all the candy I wanted."

The snort told me she rejected my theory. However, her eyes betrayed her. That had hit home.

"I came out here to answer a question: how involved you are with this woman. The answer is, very. Is it guilt, or is it love?"

"Oh, Miles! I wish you hadn't come here poking into all of this. I feel like I'm being crushed between two opposing forces. I love you, but I feel guilty about what I've done to her. I don't think it's blinded me to her."

"It's not like I've been digging for dirt on her. It seems to fall into my lap. The fact the horse was electrocuted—"

"Not fact. The mink farmer's claim, based on months-old memory," Jane stated.

"True." I met her guarded gaze. "But what about Babs's suggestion that Georgia drugged Fury to affect his performance, leading Megan to decide to move him to another barn? Was this the action of a pissed-off Georgia, who knew her status had changed to ex-lover? Or was it Megan's paranoid imagination?"

"You know how twisted newly broken-up lovers can be. I'd guess that was the case." Jane jabbed the gardening fork in the rich, dark dirt. The action seemed a little vigorous to me.

"Which? Both of them were new exes."

"Megan acting paranoid."

"Oh? Not that Georgia actually drugged the horse?"

"That's so farfetched, Miles."

"Am I making up the fact the two horses were switched?"

"All of it circumstantial or hearsay."

"This isn't a court, Jane." I took a couple of breaths to give us time to defuse. "I'll tell you what. The test takes three days. Until we hear back with DNA established proof of the identity of Wyatt/Fury, I'll drop all this. Okay?"

She came to me, muttered something against my chest, which I took to be agreement, put her arms around me, and we did some mutual comforting. I felt detached, though.

Jane said, "I think a part of this, my being freaked out, is that I'm feeling crowded on my own turf. You're pushing so hard to solve this I'm afraid there's going to be a casualty. Someone innocent. Or our relationship."

"Did you really mean what you said about wishing I'd never come?"

"Oh, Miles." The words were more vibration than sound as they filtered to me through my chest.

Not a real answer. I thought about giving both Jane and me a little space. There was that motel down the road from Putney.

CHAPTER THIRTEEN

The motel room was tiny with a fetid residue from smokers. I had a compact blue car from Rent-a-Wreck on the stingy side for legroom. And my heart shriveled down to match.

Being here had seemed the wise thing to do.

I got a road map for Maine and found Blue Hill. I traced the back roads with my finger, imagining a winding solo trip among the lobsters and coastal cliffs. Folded the map up and put it back in my bag. It made me too lonely. Besides, I'd end up spending money I didn't have and would have to find out of the blue when the credit card bill arrived.

I didn't think I was ready to just walk away from the murder of Megan. Or Jane, for that matter. Fortunately I had Victoria. She "dropped by" and invited me to groom for her at an event she'd entered. I said, "Sure. Why the heck not? I'd just as soon polish your boots and brush your horse as stay in this little room. But I don't know the first thing about braiding your horse's mane or tail."

"Not to worry, that'll be done. Georgia has someone come to the barn the day before to do that. Night will have to wear a nylon-lined blanket and have her tail tied up in a bag. I'm sure she will love that."

I laughed and nodded to think of Night dressed to the horse nines.

"I'm riding in the first group at the ultra basic level. My daughter will ride at the next level, Preliminary. She will probably hang out with the other Stoneleigh-Burnham riders, and I'll only get glimpses of her from a distance. I wasn't going to ask anyone."

"But here I am with time on my hands."

Vic smiled. "Something like that. If you can be ready tomorrow morning at six thirty, I'll swing by and pick you up. Georgia's hauling my horse with Naomi's, so we'll go in my car."

"All right, but you're getting bargain basement help." I shook my head with a small grin. "I'd like to see that black mare go through her paces."

The next morning Vic arrived with damp hair, a small white paper bag, and two large cups of French roast coffee from the Putney general store. From the bag was my choice of sticky sweet rolls. The sight of food made my stomach flip. I took the coffee and called it good.

Victoria's outfit for the morning consisted of light gray riding breeches, which came to the bottom curve of her calf, and mismatched socks with high-top sneakers. Over her white shirt, she wore a yard-sale sweatshirt decorated with jolly California raisins.

"You'll have to tell me what you want me to do," I said, scrunched in the car. I struggled to get awake after a night of tossing and turning and thinking about a road trip to Maine.

"I hired you because you are experienced." Vic laughed.

"I'm as smart about combined training as Jane was about roping." I knew Vic had been told, in detail, about Jane's initiation into real Western living, because I'd been in my living room at the ranch when Jane called her up. Vic and I were in stitches while Jane related roping that three-hundred-pound calf from the ground and being dragged through every cow pie in southwest Montana. I could hear Vic's hoots over the phone line all the way from Vermont.

I was glad to have Jane's best friend for company, although remembering this intimate time at the ranch stabbed my guts. I felt closer to Jane being around Vic, and she reminded me that Jane did have horse sense when it came to friends. Yet it did make me wonder about her misplaced feelings of loyalty to Georgia.

Was it loyalty? Or guilt for her selfish betrayal? Was she falling in love with that long, cold drink of water? I wished I knew, because if Jane really didn't want me anymore, if she just didn't know how to tell me, then I should get the hell out of here for my own good. But I never was one to give up on a project too early. Someone would have to tell me to butt out. And that someone would have to be my girl, Jane.

By the time we pulled onto the grounds at the Stoneleigh-Burnham girls' school, the caffeine had kicked in big-time. My feelings were churning, stoked with memories and longing for the way we were. As she pulled into a parking slot, Victoria began a nervous chatter about this day's ride, whetting my interest in watching Night and Vic do their thing.

Victoria signed in and received her competition number on a bib and one corresponding number for the horse's bridle. I, as her Sherpa, walked beside her to the trailer parking area. Vic was saying, "I need to walk the cross-country jump course because our division will be first, and I don't want to try and fit it in between the dressage test and my time to start the course."

"I'll take your stuff to the van," I offered.

"That would be great," Vic said, handing me her shiny, tall black riding boots, helmet, and a jacket in a cleaner's bag to add to her satchel that I already carried. "But don't look for the van. Georgia brought the three-horse slant."

I pointed out Naomi, alone at the first jump of the cross-country phase. She stepped off the distance approaching the jump, and Vic explained to me that a rail would be added to heighten the jumps in Naomi's division.

"I'll join her. Maybe some of her smarts will rub off on me," Vic said. She looked at her wristwatch. "Meet me at the trailer at nine fifteen. Okay? That blue and silver one."

Victoria indicated one parked on the far side of a field, and I made my way toward it. Lettering on the side claimed it to be from North Winds Farm. As I approached I heard voices.

"No! Georgia, really." This was Jane's voice.

I stepped a little faster. When I got to the rig, I hung Vic's coat on the sideview mirror of the truck and set the satchel and boots on the hood. The ramp on the trailer had been let down and the horses, white and black, were tied to opposite sides of the trailer. As I rounded the white rump, I again heard Jane's distressed voice. What I saw flabbergasted me. I thought only guys did this with women. Georgia had Jane's wrists pinned over her head to the inside wall of the horse trailer, and she pressed the full length of her body against her.

Georgia's words cut through the absurdity of the scene. "You *must*, Jane. I can't live without you."

I said on my way up the ramp, "You'll be lucky to live at all when I get through with you."

I spun her around by the tweed jacket material across her shoulders, grabbed her tie in one white-knuckled hand, and looked deep into her eyes. "If Jane doesn't want your attentions," I drew this word out, long and slow, "then back off."

I shoved her toward the ramp. She slipped on some bright green horse manure and fell. The horseshit greased her trip down the ramp. When she staggered to her feet at the bottom, her white shirt and wheat jeans outfit had been revamped half white and half green, like jester's clothes. Her natty tweed jacket looked a bit rumpled, too.

Georgia looked down in disbelief, then shot her sharp-faceted sapphire gaze at me. "You *bitch*."

I verged pretty strongly on wanting to wipe her face in the horse manure, too, but Jane clasped my forearm with her firm hand. "Stay," she whispered.

I looked at her. A smile, struggling to escape, played in her eyes. In that look, all my fears dissolved. She was mine. Had never been Georgia's. And she had just had an education in Georgia that had put that guilt of hers in perspective. While Georgia sputtered and fumed, Jane said, "You've made your point, I think." Her voice was soft.

"Let's blow this Popsicle stand," I said, placing her hand on my arm.

CHAPTER FOURTEEN

Georgia's explosive Worchester swearing reached like a long shadow across the competitor parking. The words cut off abruptly mid-"fuck," when she seemed to realize how loud she was and how that might play out. I indulged in a few moments of delicious fantasy: Georgia in a rage, trying to sponge off her breeches and enlarging the mess to a green-brown smear.

Jane's hand rested on my right forearm. "Now I'll need to address you as sir, I expect."

"You'll have to explain that one."

"My knight in shining armor. You will be Sir Miles from now on." Jane smiled up at me. Her brindle brown eyes were playful. "I've been a fool to protect her, believing that you were attacking her out of jealousy."

"Why, there was some of that."

"It wasn't love, it was guilt. If you knew the full scope of the guilt I carry…"

"A powerful emotion. One that motivates too many twisted actions." I lifted a rope at the edge of the car park for Jane to slip under, then followed. We were now in the area for spectators near the start of the cross-country segment, the second of the three phases.

In contrast to all the action around the vans and trailers, this part of the grounds seemed deserted. No horses had started on the cross-country course. Then it hit me. "Vic! I'm grooming for her. She's one of the first levels of competitors, and I've got to help her get ready. Georgia will shoot me if I go near the rig."

"She'll need some time to recover her poise after that little incident. I wouldn't worry about her hanging around, looking like she does. Georgia will be on her way back home to change her clothes. We'll have a clear field through the rest of dressage, then the change in tack and gear for the cross-country. Georgia will be back before the stadium jumping, though. We'll have to figure out how to help Victoria through that. Naomi won't have any trouble with Georgia tending to her. At least no more than usual."

"I can take Vic's change in tack and outfit for the third phase to her car and change her there," I said.

"That would work. Let's go find her. She should be coming off the cross-country course by now. Wasn't she walking it with Naomi?"

"Yes. Can you do whatever Naomi needs? The stuff Georgia would have done for her?" I squinted. "I don't even have a clue."

At that moment, we saw Victoria at the timber jump made from six stacked logs, the last obstacle of the Novice course that she and Night needed to negotiate. Her concentration was intense as she stood by the jump, yet to be raised another twelve inches once the Novice had passed. Vic studied the footing on the landing side, then spun and walked back with long steps, measuring off the number of horse strides in the approach.

I turned to Jane and held her arm. "Let's not tell Vic or Naomi about what happened. Hearing about that would be distracting and a downer."

"You're right." Jane looked at her watch. "Georgia will be back in about two hours. I'll meet up with Naomi when she finishes walking the course."

"Why is it taking her so long?"

"She has thirty-five obstacles at her Advanced level. There's a whole loop that she takes in addition to Vic's course. The jumps are three foot eleven, with some of the drop jumps six foot eleven inches, some landing in water."

"What about Vic? How many jumps does she have to take?"

"She rides Beginner Novice and must jump fifteen jumps at two foot seven inches."

"Rugged."

"You said it. Never interested me. Too many people die or are crippled for life in this sport from a horse catching its knee at the top of a jump and somersaulting over on the rider or some other devastating variation. Those somersaulting falls are often lethal to horse or rider. They are called rotational falls."

"Like Superman."

"Right. Like Christopher Reeves. You know, in just two years, thirty-seven eventing riders died."

"Jeez, that's terrible. What about the horses?"

"Sometimes the horse gets up and gallops away. All too often, they don't. This information is hard to get at, but at least nineteen top-level horses were killed or destroyed due to injuries during that 2007 and 2008 period."

"Can't something be done to keep that from happening?"

"Course and jump design have changed lots over the years to try to minimize injuries. One of the improvements is frangible pins, which give way when the impact from the horse is too great. But many of the jumps don't have them." Jane barked an ironic sort of laugh. "At the upper levels, they actually grease the front of the horse's leg, both fore and hind, hoping it will help a horse slide off the jump."

"Does Georgia do that for Naomi?"

"I don't know."

All this information hit me like an icy waterfall. "This is crazy. Why do people put themselves and their horses through this…" I hesitated. "Sport?"

"Maybe it's just that, the danger. Like skydiving."

"Hey, guys." Victoria walked up to us.

Jane looked at her watch. "We don't have a lot of time before you're up for dressage."

"Which ring are the Novices using?" I followed Vic's gaze and could see from this slight rise that of the four dressage rings, one of them was already in use.

"The one on the far left. That larger one is for the advanced division, Naomi's. I'd better hurry."

"See you later." Jane waved.

"While you're in the dressage ring, Vic, I'll gather all your gear, and we'll change for the next phase at your car," I said as we headed for the trailer and her waiting horse.

"Why the change? Did something happen with—"

"Yes, but I'll tell you later."

"Mysterious. You have my car keys?"

"No, you still have them."

Vic did some self-patting down and came up with the keys hiding in an inside zipper pocket of her jacket.

"Let's get cracking."

I got Night groomed and saddled while Vic spruced up in her white breeches and black coat. Vic tied her stock tie and fastened it with a pin, like a gold safety pin. I dutifully held the mirror. "What's the point of that get-up? Why not just a tie?"

Victoria laughed. "It would be simpler. This harkens from

the days when it was a handy bandage, and the safety pin was practical. Now it's tradition."

Jane and Naomi arrived just as I did the final once-over on Night with a slightly oiled cloth to bring up her shine. When Victoria bounded into the saddle, I buffed each tall black boot with the same cloth.

"Go get 'em, Tiger," I whispered. Just for Vic, I let my corny side show. She gave me back a first-class wink. After Vic rode off, I turned to see if I could help Naomi and Jane.

"We have plenty of time. He likes me to do this for him." Naomi brushed her milk-white steed and polished his coat with a soft cloth. I could see her hands shake. I thought maybe it calmed her to touch her horse. She placed the saddle and gently set the girth. A tiny manure stain on one hind foot stood out, so I got the can of baby powder and sprinkled some on the spot, effectively erasing the stain. He looked good.

"I hope I get to see you ride. Be a treat, I expect."

All I got from Naomi was half a smile.

"You nervous?"

She looked me straight in the eye and gave a twist to her lower lip. "Always." Jane held her coat for her, Naomi slipped her arms in, adjusted her black shadbelly coat. I gave her a leg up onto her nearly seventeen-hand horse.

"Probably the thing that gives you an edge," I said. "Does it disappear by the time you enter the ring?"

"Usually. Thanks, you guys, for everything."

I watched her ride to the warm-up area. I couldn't imagine a more stunning frame, her dark skin contrasting the white horse and her white breeches. She wore a black top hat, as was the custom at her upper level.

Jane helped carry all Vic's gear to the car and load it in the trunk. As I shut the trunk I asked, "What's your plan?"

"I've got to get everything laid out and ready for Naomi. Do you have Vic's body protection and her medical armband?"

I must have looked as baffled as I felt. "Armband?"

"In case she is hurt on the course, all of her medical information is readily available. I'm sure it is in her bag."

"I knew about the body armor, but the armband is creepy."

"Saves a lot of time wondering what blood type a rider is, or if they have allergies to drugs. Required equipment now."

"I'll make sure. Remember our two-hour estimate. I'd hate to have Georgia show up before you get Naomi changed."

Jane stood on her tiptoes and gave me a kiss. "Don't worry. I plan to keep an eye out for her."

CHAPTER FIFTEEN

Oh, it was a disaster!" Victoria burst out, laughing when she rode up to me. She kicked her stirrups free and lay out along Night's neck, hugging the mare. "She was great, though. I was the one who made a mess of it."

"Were you eliminated?"

"No. Just the highest accumulation of dressage fault points possible, I'd warrant." Victoria flung one leg over and slid off the tall mare. She gave Night a couple of firm pats on the neck. "All my doing, of course."

"Let's not worry about any of that now. The car's over there." I pointed.

When we got to the car, I handed Vic her clothes bag. She got out of her riding jacket, then got in the backseat to change into her polo shirt. I handed her Night's reins through the open window and stripped the dressage saddle off the mare. The horse was cool and dry. I placed the jumping saddle on her back on top of a quilted pad and buckled shin boots on her front legs, securing them with a strip of blue duct tape.

Vic emerged from the car with armband in place and her body protection vest and helmet ready to go on. I helped her with those things. She looked at Night. "Let's take the braids out of her mane. Give me something to grab if I need to." We set to work with scissors to cut the thread securing the twenty or so braids along the mare's neck, and pulled the hair apart.

"Spoils the look," I said, eyeing the kinky mane flying in all directions.

"Wild. Like her." Vic scratched the horse behind her ears. Night lowered her head and pressed her forehead against Vic's chest.

"Is that everything?" I stood back and looked at them together. Vic's long-sleeved polo shirt and protective vest were blue with black stripes, and Night's saddle pad was the same blue with three silver stars on the corner. "Quite a turnout."

"My number bib. I think it's…"

"Here it is." I handed it to her with the armband and removed the small disc number from the dressage bridle, then attached it to the snaffle bridle crownpiece. Vic put the number bib over her head, and I tied the strings at her waist. "I think that's it."

Vic snugged the girth, and I boosted her up. "Wish me luck." Vic had this wonderful ear-to-ear grin, a bit on the sardonic side. "I have a while to limber up before my number will be called."

"I won't say 'break a leg.'"

"No! Please don't."

"But good luck. She'll take care of you." I put my hand on her boot top. "Look, Victoria. Be careful. Jane told me about how many riders and their horses are injured in this sport."

"I will. This may be my big hurrah, and next year I'll just do what I love the most. Poking along on the trails."

"Come out and visit me sometime. I'll show you some trails."

"You are on, my girl," Vic said.

When the two rode off, I followed aimlessly in their wake for a short way, then remembered Naomi might be doing her dressage. That would be something to watch.

An enormous bay paint was in the large dressage ring when I joined the scattered, hushed spectators. He was flawless, strong and obedient, though a little heavy on his feet. A lean brown thoroughbred with lots of poise but not much flash was next. The rider frowned and hunched his shoulders the whole time, not making a pretty picture. Both horses, the riders giving almost invisible signals, executed the pattern perfectly. They changed from trot to canter, the circles exactly formed at the letters along the rail, and traversed the long rectangular ring on the diagonal. The tracks in the dirt overlaid each other, showing against the harrowed surface.

A white flash crossed the corner of my eye. Moving at a strong trot, Naomi and her beautiful horse came into view from behind the horse trailer sheltering the judges, approaching the far end of the ring and the entry point. Naomi circled wide and entered the ring dead center, down the middle to the X point, came to a balanced halt, and she saluted the judges.

What I saw that day changed my view of riding forever. Dressage had always been like watching paint dry. But these two, horse and rider, moved in the ring like they were silk, or perhaps mist with sun cutting through. The light, soft communication between the pair was offset by the arched neck power of the horse. And when they left the ring, I saw a second thing I'd never seen or heard of happening before: all the spectators sitting on the grass rose to their feet and clapped. While I stood there, dazed, the next poor soul entered the ring. They did everything in a practiced, lackluster manner, turning in a performance to forget.

I wandered across the hill to the cross-country course to

see if Vic and Night had queued up to start yet. They were ready for the timer, third in line, and I watched while they set off at an easy canter for the first jump. I hoped the horses didn't find the jumps as spooky as I did. Brightly colored squash ranged along the takeoff lines, and corn stalks rustled and swayed at each side. Night took the first jump effortlessly.

After that, I walked up a long rise where a bunch of spectators sat in chairs along the top. I figured they knew where the best view was. I joined them. Everything had a vibrant edge: the vivid green of the grass, yellow and orange pumpkins and squash, the riders' bright polo shirts and hat silks. Horses heading for the finish line had lines of white sweat along their necks where the reins rubbed, their nostrils red on the inside and the blow of breath through their noses sounding like freight trains. These were all the Novice entries heading for home. Some of them could have been on fitter horses.

Night was somewhere out on the course when the last horse in Novice started on course, and behind him the fence crews raised the jumps from two feet seven inches to three feet seven for Preliminary.

I decided it was time to head back, though I had hoped to see Night and Vic take their last few jumps. I wasn't in that much of a rush because I knew Vic needed time to cool the mare down and let her unwind before the stadium jumping phase.

Nearing the start and finish gates, I saw Jane. Naomi circled her horse at a slow trot, warming up. Jane and I must have caught sight of each other at the same time because she waved her hand at me, and I felt this queer sense of relief. I hadn't realized until then that I was worried Georgia would return before we were ready for her. So, what would she do? I could handle her.

Naomi's colors for her polo shirt, silk cap cover, and horse accessories were yellow, red, and orange. The colors brought a certain African feel of gutsiness and life to the team.

Jane walked up to me. "Did you get to see Naomi?"

"I will never forget that till the day I die."

"I wondered if you'd seen the ride. Here comes Vic."

We both cheered them over the finish line. "They look good. She's smiling, and the horse looks fit."

"Yeah, I don't think she smiles unless she's having fun."

Vic spotted us and called out, "Clean run!"

"Great." I pointed toward the car, and she nodded that she'd understood. I said to Jane, "I think she got a bunch of penalties in the dressage. She didn't have time to tell me why."

"Yes. I was there. Have to tell you about it later. Vic may have some overtime penalties on the cross-country. Who cares? She's doing a great job."

We heard Naomi's number called and looked in time to see her leave the start box and gallop up the hill to the first jump.

"If she takes all of them like that, she's home free. Let's go back to Vic's car. She'll join us when she has Night cooled down," Jane said.

"Wish I could watch them all the way around. This turns out to be pretty thrilling."

"Now that Naomi's on the cross-country phase, I'm out of a job. Georgia should be back at any time, and she can get her ready for the next phase. Did you bring any lunch?"

"Vic packed one. It's in the cooler on the backseat." I looked around, "They too high-toned here for a concession stand? A tube steak or something, cup of hot coffee?"

"I guess." Jane laughed. "I know you love your hot dogs."

"Admit it, you like 'em, too." I gave her a half smile.

After we'd all had lunch and laughed at Victoria's retelling of her cross-country round, we got her ready for the stadium jumping and took our time leading Night over to the ring with all the brightly colored jumps.

"If I can just manage a clear round here, I might save face," Vic said.

"Take your time and keep your head. This horse could do it with a sack of flour tied to her back."

"Gee, thanks, Jane." Vic brushed her stringy blond hair to one side and put on her helmet. I gave her a leg up and Vic rode away to do her warm-ups.

Jane and I leaned on the split rail fence around the jumping area and watched a few other Novices negotiate the final phase of the horse trials. It was easy from this side of the rails to fault the riders with too rapid an approach, or one with not enough impulsion to carry the horse up and over, or simply a bad setup. What amazed me was how game and athletic the horses were. Often they made the riders look good and covered their mistakes by heroic action. But some weren't so lucky, and the horse refused or hit the top rail. "Lowering the height of the fence" was what they were penalized for. They could knock everything down under the top rail and not have a fault, if that was possible.

My heart leaped against my rib cage when Vic entered the ring. Night looked alert and energetic. They circled once and then went between the start poles.

Jane spoke at my side, "The pace is good. Steady approach. God, what a jumper that horse is! Vic is doing a great job riding the mare. I'm proud of her."

We looked at each other briefly. "Me, too. I'm keyed up about this." I laughed. "Maybe it's because I'm her groom."

"I'm sure that's why." Jane rolled her eyes.

Vic rode smoothly from one jump to the next, an in-and-out, with one stride between, and then the chicken coop and a set of four poles in an upright. We knew ahead of time she'd have trouble here because the setup was just a little off. I felt Jane's hand cover mine, and yes, the top pole rolled off.

"Four points," Jane whispered.

The two of them finished the round with no more mishaps. Vic's eyes were a little wild as she crossed the finish line. We met them at the out gate.

"Oh, my God! What an ordeal!" Vic said.

"You did it, Vic." Jane took the reins at the bit to lead Night away from the excitement of the gates. Vic turned it over, her hands hanging at her sides.

"Four points, that's all," Jane said.

"I know, but if you add those to the ones I got in the dressage ring, you'll be amazed." Vic lay full forward on Night's neck. "I promise we won't do any more of this for a while," she whispered in the proximity of the mare's ears, her voice husky.

The flash of photography strobes arrested my attention. Vic had the best view from the top of Night, but we all looked over to a truck marked KBRTV with a light focused on Georgia Farmer. She had a funny look on her face halfway between annoyance and gratification. We went a little closer, joining a small knot of listeners.

"I have with me today a star trainer in the horse world. Her protégée, Naomi Bly, has just finished a clear round in the second phase of these Horse Trials at Stoneleigh-Burnham School, after turning in a flawless dressage round. What do you have to say about that Georgia?"

"This is a superb rider who I know you'll see next year at the Olympic Games. She's worked hard under my tutelage and turned in an excellent two rounds. We have yet to see her make the stadium—"

The reporter interrupted Georgia with that phony sadness

they reserve for plane crashes and mass shootings. "Could you tell us about the other rider who you had put so much store in? Megan Fisk, who died in a tragic—"

Georgia looked around, seeking a safe place. "No, I've got to help Ms. Bly."

"Didn't Megan die in your barn?"

"Leave me alone!" Georgia straight-armed the microphone into the interviewer's chest, and then shoved her to one side. "This interview is over."

"Wait! Ms. Farmer! We'd like—"

"I don't give a damn."

CHAPTER SIXTEEN

Victoria, Jane, and I were at the barn after the big event. Jane disappeared up the stairs to the loft and dropped hay down into Night's feeder. Vic fussed over the mare. We were a team, a flock of friends, rubbing Night down, fluffing the sawdust in her stall and cleaning tack. All of my favorite smells in one place. Well, maybe not all.

Victoria cooed over her horse. "You are the most beautiful horse in the world. And the most talented."

Jane winked at me. "Did you ever think anyone would say that about this mare?"

Oh, how she could stir me up with just a wink. Hard to believe. I smiled to watch the two longtime friends. I sat on a hay bale in the aisle, cleaning Victoria's saddle and bridle, and we were laughing and girling it up. Jane was with me now. All the way. I mentally took the rental car back and threw away the map of Maine.

Victoria had put the kettle on to heat up in the tack room earlier, and now we heard the whistle. Victoria fetched the boiling water to make a bran mash for Night. She came back toward us saying, "How dumb was that woman to get rude to a news reporter? So, tell me again about the scene with Georgia and the horse trailer. And don't leave anything out." Vic did a very good Lily Tomlin snort while stirring the hot water into the bran, molasses, and cut-up carrots.

"I can't believe the way she acted," Jane said.

I could, but I didn't have to rub it in. "Georgia doesn't know how close she came to becoming the Jolly Green Giant."

"Amazing." Vic shook her head while she placed a gunnysack over the mash to let it steam. "I never imagined women behaving that way."

"Guess anyone can be a butthead," I observed. "Georgia seemed to think no one could resist her charms. You know, Naomi told me about the pass Georgia made at her. Pretty crude there, too. Naomi thinks Megan was mad as hell at Georgia."

"Yes, I was surprised at the total lack of finesse. And so pleased my knight rode up at the right time." Jane smiled at me.

"So, where do you go from here, Vic?" I put the tack over an empty stall door and sat on a hay bale put there for the outside horses. I stretched my legs out ahead of me and crossed them, balancing on one heel of my city boot. "The Rolex? Or will it be Olde England for you?"

"What I really wish I could do is go back to 4-H or Pony Club. More my speed. They won't let me in, though. I think the cutoff age is eighteen."

"Look what you've done in three months. I'm impressed," said Jane.

"I did well today, didn't I? The one exception was that little mental breakdown in the dressage ring," Vic said, laughing at the memory. She punctuated her statement by shooting the bolt home on Night's stall door. "Maybe I don't take it seriously enough."

Jane covered her mouth, and then she burst out in laughter,

too. "Yes, I think I'd never laughed so hard, once I got over the shock."

"I tried not to notice you sitting over there on the grass," Vic said, making a rude sound.

"You forgot the pattern you were supposed to ride, didn't you?" Jane lifted the cover on the bran mash and slipped her hand in to check the temperature.

"What was your first clue?" Victoria smiled with an ironic twist.

"I've never seen anyone do what you did when you realized you were hopelessly wrong," Jane said. "The elegance with which you rode into the center of the ring, bowed hats off to the judges, while laughing your fool head off. Your good humor made everyone laugh, too."

"Yeah, it's so proper and hush-hush watching dressage riders all alone in the test ring. Makes me want to fart."

"Miles!" Jane said, shocked and cackling.

I grinned at her and noticed movement down at the far end of the shadowy aisle. Placing the bridle down, I slowly stood.

Jane froze, watching me. She whispered, "What is it?"

"Maybe a cat." But I knew if that was true, it was mighty tall.

I left our lighted end of the barn, moving slowly down into the dark aisle, listening. Who was lurking around, trying to hear our conversation? I thought Georgia had left almost immediately after dropping off the two horses, but maybe she hadn't. Naomi had followed the horse trailer and made sure her horse was comfortable, then left. I'd seen her drive away half an hour ago. Had Arthur been in the office, and we hadn't seen him? Or was he hanging out in one of the nearby horse's stalls? Or was this sneaky Pete someone else?

Now that we three cackling women had become mute, the

only sounds were the soft rustles of horses stirring in their stalls and the regular grinding of teeth on hay. Halfway down the aisle, I came to an intersection with a wash rack on the left and a dark doorway to the right. I remembered this led out to the manure dump, a concrete enclosed pit. I froze, checking each minute sound. Perhaps the shadow person had gone through the wash area and down the other aisle. I turned left toward the wash rack, stopping to listen every step or two. I came to the next main aisle and looked both ways. No movement other than horse faces looking at me over the stall doors. No sounds except the soft blow of a horse exhale, the contented chewing of tame horses.

Lights! Where was the switch? I groped the unfamiliar wall. I turned and went back to the door, which opened to the outside.

A tabby cat meowed and pushed her way in through the partially open door out to the manure pit. When she spotted me, she purred, arched her back, and rubbed herself on the edge of the door.

Now that my eyes had become accustomed to the half-light, I saw a line of switches on the wall to my right. I flipped them all on at the same time, then opened the door to the manure dump and thrust my head out, not expecting to see anyone.

I did. There, out on the manure pile was Arthur, seized in motion like a coyote in the headlights. He looked furtively around, and I had the sense he was crouched and ready to run. I felt more than saw Jane and Victoria come up behind me. Jane put her hand on my shoulder, and I could hear her breathing.

"What's going on, Arthur?" I asked.

"You shouldn't be here," was his big response. He jammed the manure fork deep into the pile and leaned on it, like he had a right to be there, and we didn't. *On the manure pile, for Christ's sake.* He looked down with a sullen frown.

Jane stepped around me. "Arthur, what are you doing out here in the dark with a manure fork?"

Suddenly I knew. He was burying something.

CHAPTER SEVENTEEN

I jumped down off the wheelbarrow ramp on to the soft, warm composting manure.

Arthur jerked the manure fork out and leveled it at me. "Stay where you are."

I almost laughed, but he was serious and I stayed.

"Arthur. You can't hide this. Whatever you're trying to cover up will come out anyway." I looked at him like I had some authority, and shook my head.

Jane spoke in a crisp voice. "If you don't step back, put the fork down, and let us see what you are burying, I will call the police."

He looked for a way out of this, unwilling to give up. In the end, he got smart, shoved the fork deep into the steaming manure, and stepped back to the concrete wall mumbling, "None of your business."

He had sunk the fork so firmly, it was hard to jerk out. I did on the second try, and then moved to where I'd first seen him. "What's in here, Arthur?"

He kept his eyes down, a disdainful curl to his lips. Sliding the fork parallel to the surface, I flipped the manure off in shallow layers. My stomach was a little queasy, not knowing what I would find.

Jane and Victoria approached, being careful not to block the strong beam of the floodlights. I stood at the bottom of a foot-deep crater. There wasn't anything there. After a minute or two Vic said, "Maybe that's not the exact spot."

I shot a glance over to Arthur and caught his quick smile disappearing. I decided to work in a five-foot circle with my first excavation in the center, asking Vic and Jane to step off five feet and mark the outside distance. I checked my decision against Arthur's expression and knew I was on the right track. First I had to shift the ring of built-up manure I'd transferred from the crater. I tossed each fork full as far as I could. Once again, I began the measured, slow layer-by-layer removal of bedding and horse manure.

The tines clanked against a solid object. Carefully, I raked the manure and sawdust away, then slid the tines underneath and lifted it up to the light. Here was King Arthur in a can. I chuckled remembering all the phone calls to smoke shops I'd made as a kid, thinking I was so funny and original. "Do you have King Arthur in a can? You'd better let him out."

Jane took the can and brushed it clean. Gingerly, she opened the lid. Inside were papers, which she removed and inspected. "These are photocopies of checks. But I can't quite see who…What on earth are you doing trying to hide this?"

"My personal records," Arthur said with a smug smile.

I snorted. "Most people use desks to file their papers. What's so special about these?"

"The light's too dim to see who made these checks out or for how much. Are you the payee, Arthur?" Jane held one of them toward him. He snatched at it, and Jane jerked it back.

Vic said, "Let's go inside so we can get a better look at them." We trooped to the door, stamping the manure off our feet, sounding like a herd of buffalo. I turned the outside light off, went around the corner, and just about jumped out of my skin. Georgia was standing, bigger than life, in the aisle. The light from above cloaked her face in darkness.

"What are you doing here?" she demanded.

Vic stepped forward. "We were putting my horse away. Is there a problem with that?"

"Oh? Are you bedding her down on the manure heap?"

Jane and I stood shoulder to shoulder with Arthur a close second. "Georgia," Jane said, "what's the problem?"

"I saw every light in the barn on and walked down from the house." She must have spotted the King Arthur can, because she stepped forward and grabbed it out of Jane's hand. She flipped the lid up and pulled the papers out. "What's going on here?"

I thumbed to my rear, keeping my eyes on her. "He had it. Is it yours?"

Georgia got a good look at the papers and her face froze. "Oh." She stuffed them back into the can, aiming her gaze over our shoulders at the shrinking Arthur. "Arthur, go to bed. You have to be up at five o'clock. I've told you not to socialize with boarders."

"I heard them talking, and came to—"

"Hardly socializing," Vic said.

"Never mind." Georgia looked at the three of us. "Now if you would be so kind, it's time to leave." She shoved the tobacco can into the side pocket of her canvas barn coat.

Jane spoke up. "Just a minute, Georgia. Those are Arthur's records, and you have no right—"

"I'll give them back to him in the morning."

As Arthur sidled past me, I felt his hand searching for mine. I had an absurd flash that he was making a pass at me, but then he pressed a thin, hard object into my hand. He caught my eye and gave me a tight half wink to let me know something meaningful had just happened. I slid the thing into my jeans pocket.

Georgia herded us out, and then she turned the outside lights off before we'd reached our cars. We crunched across the gravel.

I whispered to Vic, knowing that Jane was too far to hear. "We've got to talk…meet someplace. I'll bet she's watching."

At her car Vic said, "Listen, I could eat a horse—oops. How 'bout a side of beef?"

"Have to be cooked? How 'bout you, Jane?"

She nodded and whispered, "Let's get the hell out of here. Follow me. We'll meet at a café in Putney."

We drove off in our separate cars, Vic and I together and Jane leading on the half-hour drive down the interstate to Putney. On the way, Vic and I talked about how rude Georgia was when the TV reporter was interviewing her.

"She won't get many students that way. What does she think? It's okay to be rude, but not okay to be a lesbian?" Victoria said.

I shifted in my seat and stretched my legs out. "I'd guess." I didn't tell Vic about the young Georgia's experience at the summer camp. That was up to Jane.

"It's sad to think she's so scared of being outed. I wonder what worries her more, the loss of money or boarders." Vic was silent for a half breath. "Or her kids."

"What do you mean? The kids she teaches?"

Vic glanced at me with sad eyes. "All the kids she mentors. She gives them the horse attention she never got. I think it's the only love she feels."

"And they do love her. She glows around them, and they run to meet her. Funny. She's the coldest person I've ever met—away from Pony Club."

"Arthur's behavior was very weird. What all is going on? You and Jane have been keeping something from me," Vic said, eyeing me sideways.

"Not intentionally. This doesn't have anything to do with Arthur's secret bank records. I think the horses were switched. Jane and I may not agree about this, but I believe the destroyed horse was Wyatt. And, of course, so does Arthur. I mean he knows." I told her about the newspaper and my own observations about the discrepancy between the horses' markings. I added the information about the DNA sample I'd sent off for analysis. When I was finished, Vic was silent for a moment.

"What you're saying is that Megan was murdered."

"I think that's what it adds up to be. Seems off the wall, I know."

She turned her gaze on me full-bore. "I believe you're spot on. That woman has always given me the willies under my skin. Georgia is capable of anything. Is the next step going to the police?"

"Sure wish we'd seen what Arthur was hiding in the tobacco can."

Victoria nodded thoughtfully. "Something he perhaps wanted to use against Georgia."

"He hates her. And the way she treats him, by God, is it any wonder?"

"Something from the bank. An account statement, perhaps?" Vic took the Brattleboro exit. "So you think it's her account or his?"

"Wish I'd gotten a better look." I considered Vic's suggestion of going to the police with what we suspected. "We don't have anything concrete to show the authorities. But I'm going to do my damnedest to get it."

We met up at a small all-night café on the east side of Main Street. We found an empty red Naugahyde booth and settled, Jane and I opposite Vic. If my face was like theirs, we all looked on the haggard side. Up since four this morning, it was now pushing ten at night.

After we had ordered, I fished the thing in my pocket out into the fluorescent light. It was a small, flat key. I explained how it came my way. "He's got something stashed away. Do you think this is connected to the photocopies of the checks?"

"Most likely," Vic agreed. "Looks like a safe deposit key."

"Could it be a diary key?" Jane reached out and rolled it between her fingers, as if trying to get the key to speak to her.

"Shouldn't be too hard to find out where he banks and see if he has a safe deposit box," Vic said. "What's the point, though? They wouldn't let you get access."

"Why do you think he wanted me to have it? And why be so secretive about passing it to me? God, she was scary."

"I hated leaving Arthur there. Like Georgia would devour him or something," Vic said. "Once we've finished sleuthing and no longer need a reason to go to North Winds Farm, I'm moving Night someplace near here."

"What about Babs Longfellow's place? Seems to me it was closer than Georgia's facility. I liked the woman, and the place looked friendly and well run."

"That's a good idea," Jane said. "Sorry I got you into this, Vic."

"Oh, hell. What are friends for?"

❖

It was the next morning we heard that Arthur was dead. Victoria called while we were in the afterglow of lovemaking, sitting on the back patio drinking strong, dark coffee. Jane jumped when the muffled ring of her cell phone came from the deep pocket of her terry cloth robe.

"How did it happen?" Jane asked.

My ears were like a coyote's trying to catch fragmented words as though they were shreds of far away dog calls.

"Broken neck? Off the retaining wall early this morning. Oh, my."

"Who found him?" I whispered, my voice rough and hoarse.

"Oh? Did she." Jane nodded, confirming my thoughts. They talked a few minutes longer while I went to my tossed-to-one-side jeans. As I rejoined her, zipping the fly, she slipped her phone back into her pocket.

"Doesn't sound good to me, but the police say it was an accident. The wheelbarrow was partly on top of him. Must've happened early this morning."

"What do you think? Did Georgia get rid of him?" I asked Jane.

"I guess that's leaping to conclusions. It sure does look bad to me. His neck was broken. How on earth did he 'fall' off the retaining wall of the manure pit with the wheelbarrow, I'd like to know?"

"So, what do the police have to say about it? They must have some suspicions."

"They don't appear to, Miles."

"Well, I sure as hell do. Let's check him out since the police have already decided." I stood up, eager to get going.

"What do you have in mind?" Her head was turned to the side, and she looked at me askance.

I held up the small brass key Arthur had pressed into my hand last night. "Last night we talked about this. We have to find what it opens."

Jane jumped to her feet. "Give me a minute to dress."

"Where did he live?" I called out to her rapidly retreating back.

"Over the barn."

Oh, great. We got to brave the lioness in her den.

I called Vic to get her to go with us to the stables. After all, we needed some excuse to walk onto Georgia's place. She might snub me, but she couldn't refuse my entry to the grounds if I was with Jane and Victoria. Or so I thought. We set the sneak action up for the lunch hour when we hoped Georgia might be away from North Winds Stables. I wanted to check out Arthur's apartment and find out which bank he used. The three of us arrived at twelve fifteen. A new fellow, a callow youth cleaning stalls, informed us that we had just missed Georgia.

"Oh, that's too bad," I said. "We can just wait around while we watch our friend ride. Don't let us keep you from your work."

While the boy got back to cleaning stalls, Vic got Night on cross-ties to get the mare ready to ride. Jane brought Dusty over to the same side and put the saddle on him. I went outside the barn to climb the stairs running diagonally up the exterior of the barn and tried the door. It was locked.

When I got back on the ground I looked up at the hayloft, which covered most of the area of the second story. Arthur's living quarters were at one end with two little dormers. I went back into the barn, up the ladder to the hayloft, and found my way to the wall at the back, and, yes, it had a door with a simple latch. I tried it and the door opened easily onto a freakily tidy and sterile living area.

CHAPTER EIGHTEEN

Everything had a place, and each little thing was in it.
Then there was center stage. I was brought to a rigid halt
in front of a frighteningly real painting of Jesus on the cross
hanging above Arthur's bed. Only his face and torso showed.
His chest was exposed, his heart resting in lifelike detail at the
wound's opening, not the usual neat cut of the spear with two
discreet drops of blood at the lower edge.

While in the bedroom, I did a quick scan of Arthur's
closet: five neatly pressed shirts, two pair of clean work shoes
side by side, and one shiny dark blue suit. Dresser drawers
held all you'd expect. Nothing hidden in socks or beneath the
underwear.

I felt relieved to leave the bedroom and its sick painting
behind.

I didn't spend much time in the tiny kitchen. Bathroom,
ditto. Too many praying Durer hands and plain wooden crosses
for my taste. The most likely area to find something was the
desk. On the wall above the dainty but businesslike desk hung
an affair with pigeon holes, each slot marked with masking
tape: Bills, Bills Paid held the usual, phone, electric. Mail In,
Mail Out, all empty. In Bank Records-Current, I saw a short

pile. I snatched this one out of the hole and thumbed through the stack.

I made a note of the bank name and address and his account number, but I found a bonus tucked in the little pigeonhole—a tan savings book that looked like the bank had printed it before the Depression and they still had beaucoup copies. The record covered about ten of Arthur's most recent work years. The first years had entries around five or ten dollars a week. The total balance read $438.92. In recent months the entries were very different. One or two thousand at a time.

He might have had a raise, but I didn't figure it amounted to that much. This looked as though someone was paying him on a regular basis for something, like silence. Sure wasn't cleaning stalls. My convictions deepened. Arthur had photocopied the checks before depositing them, and that was what he'd stashed in his tobacco can. Had Georgia murdered him but not yet had a chance to go through his things to remove evidence of payoffs? I vacillated between taking the savings book and leaving it. Ended up putting it in my shirt pocket, tightly buttoning the flap.

The thought occurred to me that perhaps Arthur had family somewhere. He'd always struck me as a single old codger, but I might be wrong. And maybe there was a doting aunt or sibling. The desk might yet have some secrets to give up.

His filing system was as haphazardly chaotic as his apartment was anally tidy. Nothing made alphabetical sense. The file drawer on the bottom mostly held the minutiae of life, but under M was a marriage license. Arthur Warner and Alberta Farmer nearly forty years ago. Farmer. A shiver ran up my back. Could these have been Georgia's parents?

She treated Arthur like the lowest of serfs. But why on earth had he put up with her treatment? Something I needed to ask Jane about. Perhaps Georgia's drunken secret story would shed some light on this whole business.

I flipped through the rest of the alphabet. Under T, I found each year's tax filings for his entire earnings lifetime. The funny thing was, the first ten years there weren't a lot of earnings, then for ten years he listed two dependents and a whole lot of income. Fifteen years ago, he suddenly went back again to very little income and no dependents. Curious, I took a sample from each from the early days, the rich days, and recently.

Under "W" was a Washington State death certificate for Alberta Farmer. Cause of death was listed as a suicide. Moses Lake was where she had been at the time—out in the middle of the dry part of Washington, nothing but wheat fields for miles and lots of squished mice on the highways. Perhaps Alberta had relatives out there? Maybe she'd left him and moved in with family. The choice of death by suicide, if I'd been Arthur's wife, wouldn't be too big a stretch.

A car door slammed outside, and I jammed stuff back into the files, slammed the drawer, and shot out of the chair and down the ladder like nobody's business. I did a quick detour to the bathroom to regain my calm and serene exterior. When I came out of the bathroom, I saw the arrival had been a lone boarder. Since I'd left in a hurry I went over in my mind closing up the apartment to make sure I'd left it as tidy as I'd found it. I sauntered ringside to watch Victoria put Night through her paces. Jane rode over to me, kicked her stirrups free, and jumped down.

"Find anything?" she whispered.

"Lots. Tell you later." I touched my breast pocket. The book felt hot. I followed Vic around the ring with my eyes, my mind wrestling with the larger problem.

I knew the bank wouldn't let anyone but the police into Arthur's safe deposit box. But I figured we weren't quite ready to contact the sheriff. The obvious place to go from here was to search Georgia's home. Challenging, because the pseudo-Southern manse stood on a nearby hill, overlooking the stable.

❖

When we were back at Jane's, I told her what I wanted to do.

"I have to double-check some things," I said. "What are the chances of getting inside Georgia's house? The only time it might be possible to risk it is while she's away at an event or the dentist. She'll probably shoot me next time she catches me snooping around."

"You might have a chance tomorrow. Baron Von Trump is holding a dressage clinic in Woodstock. I know Vic's signed up. Georgia's going with two of her best pupils, and I thought I would take Dusty, too."

I thought about Victoria mimicking Georgia: "The Baron is top of the list, don't you know." She had put us all in stitches.

"That would be perfect."

"I'll take my cell phone and call you on the way back. You take Vic's, I'm sure she won't mind. That way if Georgia leaves early, we can warn you."

"That is a great idea. I'm not sure what I'm looking for." I froze with an idea that hit me square between the eyes. "I just remembered. You know, I think Arthur was Georgia's father."

"That's ridiculous."

"No it's not. Farmer. I saw the marriage certificate. That was the maiden name of the woman Arthur was married to.

His name is Warner. Shit, Jane. This means that Georgia's mother was Alberta Farmer and her father—"

"Oh, my God. I think she killed him." Jane looked stricken.

"Demeaned him every chance she had. I wonder why he put up with it."

Jane grew very quiet. Then she spoke in a near whisper. "I think I know why."

"Are you ready to tell me?"

Jane shook her head with a thoughtful expression. I thought it might not be long before Jane exposed the secret. "Let's look into the suicide of her mother," I said. "The article mentioned a daughter. Did Georgia have a sister?"

"No. She was an only child."

"Can we access Washington State records or newspapers in Moses Lake? You're good on the computer," I said.

"Won't be too hard to find out," Jane said. "I'll do some research while you're tossing Georgia's estate. Oh, guess I can't if I'm going to the Baron's clinic, too. Duh."

I raised an eyebrow. "You are a super woman."

"Oh, yes." Jane smiled. "I'll do the research tonight. So, Alberta, the name of a popular peach, was the inventor of the Hula Loop, the one with those rain-stick sounds. What do you think happened to all the money? Arthur sure didn't have any. Not by the look of his savings account." She handed me back the little savings book.

"Do you think Georgia's mother left all of it to her daughter and nothing to her husband?"

"That would be my guess. Buying North Winds Farm would have taken well over two million. The farm isn't that big a moneymaker, so I'd think the residue is invested for earnings." Jane lit a fire in the living room fireplace. "Chilly tonight."

"The bite of winter. I'll bet my cows are moving out of

the high country." What I wouldn't give to be pushing them low, on the back of a good horse. And Norburt. He'd be so happy we were back to being a family again, doing what he loved. I watched the flames take hold of the kindling and begin gnawing on the sweet maple logs, as my heart was gnawing for home. I reached for Jane, who nestled in beside me on the couch. Scout curled up with her nose across Jane's foot. Love warmed you like nothing in the world.

"And then her father hit some hard times and came to work for her," I said. "She took pleasure in treating him like shit. Ordering him around and insulting him every single day."

"One way to get back at him." Jane poked the fire.

"For what?"

"Ruining the first love of her life. Not to mention her own life."

"I'd say she was successful. They must have had a weird symbiotic relationship."

"Yeah, like oak and ivy. Or leeches and *The African Queen*."

We didn't laugh. It was all too sad.

"There was more." Jane's silence told me she was struggling with something fierce. This was that secret she had promised Georgia she would keep. "I don't think I can keep this confession of hers quiet any longer in the face of Arthur's death. After her parents came for her at camp, her father began sexually abusing her. He tied her up. Told her that he would fuck the queer out of her.

"He fancied himself a vehicle for God, sermonized at her and her mother for hours at a time about the evils of sodomy. Georgia was certain her mother knew about what he was doing to her. This went on until the trip Georgia took with her mother at nineteen, when she left for college in Seattle. She picked her school because of its distance from New Hampshire."

"Couldn't have gotten any farther, but no, there's Hawaii and Alaska." I shrugged. "Supposedly, her mother committed suicide. What if Georgia killed her?"

Jane nodded slowly. "Often the victim is angrier at the parent who shields the abuse than the abuser himself. She kept Arthur around to humiliate every day."

"If she killed both her parents, then it isn't any leap at all that she killed Megan. A dangerous woman, not to mention nuts."

"I was wrong to doubt your instincts on this, Miles."

"I'll only be here another few days, you know."

Jane nodded. "I'll fly out for Christmas. If you want me to?"

My heart leaped with pleasure, but I said, "Of course I do. But don't make any promises you can't keep."

"Sometimes I get so scared because there's so much land, so many miles between us. I remember watching out of the plane's window, thinking of the enormous distance..." She stood up and put another log on the fire.

"Yes, I did some of that, too." I reached for her, getting rid of the distance between us. I breathed in the sweet smell of her hair, holding her very close. "In a way, coming out here has made it harder. I see how you live, your lovely house, all the great restaurants. A place to go and dance, but mostly your friend Vic. She's wonderful. I wish I had a friend like her in Montana." I took one of those long, deep sighing breaths, fighting away the idea that it just wouldn't work to live together.

Jane turned her face up to meet mine. "I love you more than I can say, Miles." Our lips felt dry and raspy at first, needing to get reacquainted. Then, as if recognizing each other, rediscovering known places, they parted warm, moist, and soft. When Jane spoke, I was on a different plane of sensation, touch not hearing. I couldn't grasp her words at first.

"I want you to be careful when you get to Georgia's house. Check for surveillance cameras."

"I never thought about that." I was a novice. "Maybe you should be doing this," I said with a smile. "Remember when you jumped through a stall window to find out what was in Velma's barn?"

"Yes, and just about got flattened by Night. After she had been stolen and hidden in that barn, she had been cooped up too long. This is more sinister, though. We could be looking at a triple murder."

"The most dangerous people are those who think they're more clever than anybody else. I never had that problem." I gave my gal a squeeze. "I'll be careful."

"I wonder how much this whole thing hinges on Georgia's fear of being outed. The only part of her life that really seems to matter is the Pony Club. If parents pulled their kids from the barn, Georgia would crumble."

"Why, they'd be damned sure to take them out of Pony Club if the group leader was a murderess. But because she's queer? Do you think that would actually happen? Aren't people more liberated than that? Good Lord, gays could marry in Vermont, since...what's it been? Nineteen ninety-two?"

"I don't know. What matters is what Georgia believes." Jane gave me a small twisted smile. "I think I'm over my guilt for the camp episode."

"About time."

CHAPTER NINETEEN

Dawn came on little bird feet through the leaves of the maples above me. When I'd arrived at my surveillance post, it had been dark with just a skinny streak of light gold on the far horizon. Birds began singing up a storm, like they were trying out for a bird opera. The cool, fresh morning air circled into my car windows as I waited, hidden in a wooded driveway, for everyone to leave the stable area. I pulled the binoculars from the stiff leather case ready to glass them from my lookout position.

Ah, there was some action. The horse van, headlights sweeping ahead, crawled down the turn-out of the stables. Georgia, in her two-seater sports Mercedes, followed with her favorite Pony Club girl. Vic and Jane took the second girl, driving in third position so Jane could call me if Georgia turned around.

I pulled my old Timex out of my watch pocket and gave Georgia ten minutes to come back after some forgotten thing. While I waited, I tried to work on one of those sudoku things from the newspaper. There was enough light now to make out the numbers in the boxes. Didn't get very far.

When they'd been gone for twenty minutes, I started the car. I pulled up to Georgia's house and parked behind the lilac bushes without being too obvious. I walked around the manse looking for open doors and surveillance cameras. Entry proved to be more of an athletic feat than a mechanical lock-picking sort of thing. Which was a good thing, because I didn't know how to pick a lock.

The window over the kitchen sink had been left slightly open, and the screen had fallen out. I stood staring at it for a while, wondering if it was a trap. I carried one of the patio chairs below the window and scrambled up to the ledge. When you're going through a window, there's that awful point you're not sure you are going to make it, and you kick and wiggle your hind legs in the open air, inching through. With plenty of grunts, bruised elbows and scrapes, I managed to squeeze past the halfway point. I landed in a heap in the stainless sink. Fortunately, there were no dirty dishes in it.

After making so much noise coming through the window, I figured Georgia must not have a dog or a houseguest. I sat scrunched up in the sink for a bit and just listened. Funny how an empty house rustles small sounds, like a hen annoyed by strangers or a nosey dog.

I removed my boots and placed them in the sink, then began exploring Georgia's lair. The dining room table was long, with dark wood and about a dozen prissy chairs. Needlepoint cushions graced the sofa in the living space, furniture arranged in conversation-discouraging groups. I found it surprising that the public places, living room, entry hall, and downstairs washroom were spotless, Martha Stewart presentable. Unlived in, to be exact.

But the private places were in total chaos.

The bathroom off her bedroom gave me the creeps to even look through the door. Clutter covered every surface. She had toothpaste turds in the sink, and dusty, casually dropped orange peels on the carpet beside her bed. Something greenish and unrecognizable sat in a glass on the bedside table.

I stalked the hall, opening and closing doors until I found a computer room or office. I saw file drawers, but no files; everything was tossed in, the door slammed, catching the edges of some papers. The computer had a password, which I tried to break but couldn't.

In one drawer, I found about a half dozen unopened bank statements. I took them over to a chair by the window and proceeded to open them all. I wasn't very surprised to find canceled checks in the amount of the large deposits in Arthur's name. I slid out a couple and tucked them away. I dumped all the statements back into the bottom of the file drawer, covered by a mess of other papers. No need to worry about being tidy. I doubt she'd notice a dead horse in the middle of her office. I'm sure she'd just walk around it.

Back down the hall to her bedroom, I tried to find something personal, photos of girlfriends or anything. I noticed one photo of a woman with etched lines around her mouth and out from the corners of her eyes. Her hair was platinum blond. But the back of my neck felt like a spider superhighway when I saw the center of her eyes had been punched out. I guessed this might be her mother. The picture had a strange lack of intimacy about her face and the presentation, aside from the eye alteration part. I set it back on the dresser, too late realizing the visible scuff tracks I'd left on the dusty surface.

Strange that she'd put a defaced portrait of her mother at her bedside. Was it to gloat? Or perhaps a statement that she had been unseeing, or blind to what her husband had been doing to her daughter?

On one wall of the bedroom, I saw a framed graduation certificate from someplace called Exodus International honoring Georgia Farmer for completing the program. I explored the rest of the place. An entertainment room was next to the bedroom. Beside the big screen TV, I found stacks of DVDs. I smiled, not surprised to discover they were mostly of Georgia riding in shows in her youth. A couple DVDs were marked Threat Fury. I slid one of those into my pocket.

The only other photographs I found were of herself, fancily framed and displayed in the formal living room area. This was a sterile life. Everything looked so empty. Nothing else jumped out at me. I went back downstairs, shut the kitchen window to the same place it had been, got my boots, and wiped the sink. Padding to the door, I remembered Jane's warning. I couldn't see any cameras, but if I opened the door, an alarm might go off.

A thin wire leading high around the front door frame looked suspicious. I headed for the back door off the kitchen. Another tiny wire lurked along the header. But the door out to the deck didn't. Perhaps Georgia believed the two-story drop was enough to discourage entry. I slid down the Doric column in nothing flat, remembering at the last minute to take the chair I'd put below the kitchen window and place it with the others. I went back to the flower bed and smoothed out the tracks of the chair or my boots.

I had hours to kill before Georgia returned, so I searched the outbuildings. A garden shed held what all gardeners stored. The garage was locked, but I decided to give Jane's garage door opener a try.

When I was a teen with nothing to do, I'd go to Butte and hang out with the other rowdies. Our favorite thing was to drive around a subdivision in somebody's parent's car and push the garage door opener. Probably one out of five garages mysteriously opened. One time a guy was out watering his lawn when we took his door up. He turned in amazement, squirting the garage contents as the door heavily ground open.

I removed the remote from the visor, walked to the garage, and pressed the button. I had the biggest, most satisfied grin on my face as I watched the door whir up, but something hanging on a hook inside wiped that grin right off my face.

Everything rose out of my memory like a fish taking a fly. The man we had caught back in Montana last spring, the one responsible for all those horse deaths, had bragged about the wire with two alligator clips and a plug. "One clip to an ear, the other to the anus. Plug it in. Quick. No blood or mess, just a dead horse."

Here it hung. Or one just like it.

I remembered Victoria's phone, and as I stared at the wire, I unbuttoned the pearl snap on my shirt pocket and slowly pulled the phone free. Handy, this modern invention I knew nothing about, not having cell service at the ranch. Vaguely, I recalled Vic's instructions on capturing images. After a few fumbling failures, I got some good photos of the killer wire.

I left it there, closed the door, and drove back to Jane's.

CHAPTER TWENTY

That night when Jane came home from the clinic, we sat on the couch and talked into the night. She seemed reluctant to go for Georgia's throat and take what we knew to the sheriff. I asked her, "Are you still defending her? You seem to be dragging your feet about acting on this information. What do you want to do now that we've found hard evidence that she paid Arthur off, that he might have been blackmailing her, and that he was her father, and she owns an electric killer wire hanging in her garage?"

"She could just say that he wanted the money for something, a vacation to the Bahamas, and she gave it to him. But, why do you think she paid Arthur? We need to know more. Did he do the killings?"

I shook my head. "That could be, but I really doubt he killed Megan and the horse. You could tell he loved Wyatt. And let's get serious, how could he kill himself? Don't you think Arthur's aim was to damage, expose Georgia? Maybe he threatened to tell about the horse switch. Or that he was her father. That's easy to prove."

"He did tell us about the horse." Jane curled up on the couch, rooting her head under my arm so she could put her

head in my lap looking up at me. It was almost like having
Skippy here, except both Jane's eyes were brown.

"Yup. I'm sure he sent that clipping. Hedging his bets. He
had already been paid for his silence, so maybe he thought he
could leak and get away with it. Do you think she found out
he'd done that and killed him to shut him up?"

Jane was quiet a moment. "Perhaps going to the mink
farm may have alerted her to your suspicions."

"No shit, Sherlock. Or waving those bank check
photocopies around might have clued her in. If we don't
act soon, she could ditch the electrocuting wires. Purge
everything."

I felt the warm breath of her sigh against my breast. "Let's
wait to do anything until after the Quail Mountain Event.
Naomi and Victoria have both worked so hard to do well in
the event. Naomi needs to stay focused for a chance to be
selected by the Olympic Committee. And Vic? I just want her
to win her division, that's all. Sunday we'll go to the police
with everything we have and turn it over to them."

"Okay. The event is only the day after tomorrow. Saturday,
then I fly out on Monday." My body did a cold plunge. Shortly,
I'd be without her again.

❖

The next morning, when Jane logged on to her computer,
there was a message waiting from the American branch of the
registry in Louisiana.

*This is to inform you that the sample you supplied
for DNA testing can only be from the horse registered
with the Danish Warmblood Society as Threat Fury,*

number 9200643. Although we have the stallion, Dansk Vra's DNA on record to verify parental match, we also have Threat Fury's DNA on record as he has sired three foals in the part blood registry. For legal proof the sample must be obtained by an approved person.

"Dynamite! Positive proof the horses were switched," I said with jubilance to Jane. "Or at least we can get it with a new supervised sample. Ask them to send a hard copy of the results to the Brattleboro Police Department."

"I didn't know he had been a stallion."

"Probably too much of a handful if they'd left him a stud, so he was gelded. He must have sired those foals when he was a two-year-old." Most horses were gelded by the time they'd reached their yearling year, but some were progeny tested first. A stallion's coat has a higher gloss than one who has lost his testicles. Their movements and actions are prouder, more showy. Occasionally with horses where speed or brilliance counted, gelding was put off to see if they could pay attention to the rider and handler. If they were unmanageable when surrounded by other horses, it was a quick and easy fix. Snip.

"Let's watch the tape you snitched from Georgia's," Jane said.

I grew increasingly sad to see the horse and rider team of Megan Fisk and Fury do their thing. They were a beautiful team, working together in absolute concert. Here was another piece of hard evidence the horse in the video was the same as the one in the stall at Georgia's barn, posing under the name of Wyatt.

Jane wandered into the kitchen saying something about fixing some tea. After I snapped the video out of the machine, the TV went to the local channel. The noon news was on, so I sat down to watch. Suddenly I came bolt upright and shouted, "Jane! Come see this!" Georgia's face filled the screen. And lurking behind the heartiness and the wide smiles was her watchful, suspicious aspect. The background was North Winds Farm.

The reporter held the mike in the space between them. "This seemingly effortless and decisive win at Stoneleigh-Burnham Horse Trials by your protégée and student, Naomi Bly, will certainly put you on the top riding coaches of America map."

Georgia spoiled her moment by being self-satisfied and pompous. "When I first saw Ms. Bly, I knew I wanted to work with her, that she had great potential. She jumped at the chance—"

"Could you tell us about your other protégée? Megan Fisk?"

"Oh, yes. She had trouble with the pressure you encounter on the circuit. Her horse had lost the edge necessary for the top international levels." Georgia was frowning. She seemed to realize the camera was trained on her and put her happy face back on. "Ms. Bly will ride next at Quail Mountain—"

"What do you have to say about the claim that Megan killed her horse to collect on the insurance? There's a lot of speculation going on."

"That's false!" Georgia shouted into the mike. "There are no horse murderers at North Winds Farms." Her face distorted, the corners of the lips tight and turned down. Eyes slits. "It was an accident!"

"We have received information that may point to a broken romance between—"

"That's disgusting, to slander that nice girl!"

"Thank you, Ms. Farmer, who is speaking with us today

at KVNE. She is the trainer of an Olympics prospect—" The camera suddenly jolted back to Georgia. A different Georgia.

She grabbed the microphone from the reporter and yelled into it, "Take that back! You have to cut that from the interview."

The TV screen abruptly switched to a blue-suited man busy wiping a smile from his face. "And in other news…"

We stood beside each other with our mouths hanging open. "My God! She's just hung herself," Jane said, shaking her head.

"Out to dry, twisting in the wind. Makes me really want to get her."

❖

Jane spent about an hour that morning trying to find the connection to Moses Lake and Alberta Farmer. Turned out there was no family connection in Washington state. However, the archives of the local papers had a story about a mother and daughter traveling from New England to Seattle. The daughter planned on attending the university, but the sad suicide of her mother left the nineteen-year-old daughter stranded there for a week.

"Do you think it was really suicide?" Jane squinted and frowned.

"What's the alternative?" I asked without expecting an answer. I wandered off to stand and stare out the front windows. Something had been nagging at me all day. Suddenly, it hit me. I rushed back into Jane's office. "Jane! Tell me, what's Exodus International?"

"Why?" She had the most curious look on her face.

"Georgia had a completion certificate from Exodus International hanging on her bedroom wall."

"Really? That's a place that does Christian gay conversion therapy. They claim they can change any Christian's sexual orientation."

"Holy shit! You mean there are actually places that try that?"

"Yes. Parents usually send their teens at the first sign they might be gay. They're located in California. Irvine, I think."

I snorted my disbelief. "Wonder if they've ever tried changing straight to gay. I've done that myself."

CHAPTER TWENTY-ONE

Midday, we decided it would make sense to gather all our facts and information into one place, a large manila envelope. Jane wrote on the outside, "In the event of our deaths, please open." She signed it and held the pen out to me.

"How morbid. You don't really mean that, do you?"

"In truth, it started as a joke. Now I'm not laughing."

A clap of thunder resonated through the house as I took the pen and signed my name. We did laugh then, and I said, "That was on the dramatic side."

"'In the event of our deaths' isn't an easy thing to read, so I think it only fitting that we have some fanfare."

Rain hammered the metal roof, sheeting down the windows. Into the envelope went the video I'd taken from Georgia's, the DNA report, the newspaper clipping Arthur had sent, and his little savings book, plus the safe deposit box key. We had downloaded Vic's camera photos to Jane's computer and now printed off a series of the photos of the electric wire rig.

Jane added a printout of the news article about Georgia's mother's death. She said, "I'll go write up an account of the knacker's story. For non-horse people, that needs to be explained."

"Add the bit about the electric wire contraption and say what it was used for. And where I saw it, hanging on a nail to the left of her garage door. I'm sure you can tie it up in a readable story."

"I agree it needs to be put into some sort of narrative. Can you put something together for lunch? I'm famished." Jane entered her office and firmly closed the door.

I went to the kitchen, stood staring into the refrigerator for a reasonable amount of time, and then closed the door. The thought of food had been pushed down to one side. Rain pummeled the north east side of the house and was coming in. I shut the window and checked the rest of them.

The pounding rain racing out of the gutters in a runnel drew me outside. It had been a long time since it had rained this hard back home. I went out the kitchen door where the roof covered the back stairs and sat on the top stair, feeling the rain drift, smelling the fresh ozone, and watching little rivers flow down the driveway, carrying dry leaves like canoes.

When she came out an hour later, I had a noodle, bok choy, and peanut dish ready to eat.

"This is good!"

"You don't need to be so surprised. I'm a pretty good cook. That Thai restaurant jump-started me for Asian."

While I did up the dishes, Jane read to me what she'd written. The whole story was laid out. "Sounds damning, don't you think?"

Jane nodded sadly. "I know. While I was getting it all down, I got so depressed. She was one desperate woman."

"It's hard to follow, in a way, because you can't believe that anyone would be so afraid of being outed." I looked at the envelope and shook my head. "We do like to believe the myth that the whole straight world community is accepting of gays. But it is just that, a feel-good myth. And because some people in a state or community act like they accept gays, it doesn't really hide the ones who hate us and think we're God's abomination. Look at DOMA."

"That was overturned," Jane said with a puzzled look.

"What gets me," I said with some heat, "is that it was ever a law in the first place, and it took until 2013 to get rid of it."

"I agree. Putney is an open, supportive community. Around here you forget that the rest of the country can be pretty redneck."

"I think Matthew Shepherd reminded everyone in my neck of the woods."

Jane took my hand. "We're looking at 'one of us,' twisted and damaged, and that's hard to take."

"It's disturbing to see the results of the poison of homophobia, isn't it? And that her father's hatred of queers could drive him to abuse his daughter and force a poisonous religion down her throat. That the mother turned away, ignored it, perhaps even agreed." The rage subsided when I said these last words. I shook my head. "Never can quite grasp the knowledge, or maybe fact, that so many mothers turn away. Try to pretend it isn't happening to their own daughter. Or son."

"Such a perverted aspect of religion, so often combined with sexual abuse." Jane closed her eyes and sighed. "Let's not talk about this anymore. I'm getting depressed."

I grabbed her around the waist and pulled her to me, not meeting any resistance.

"I'll miss you so." I felt her lips moving against my chest, warming my wool vest.

"Yes." I steered her to the couch, and we sat down holding each other all the while. "It would be nice if love had no complications."

She snuggled against me like a cat. Maybe when I got

back home, I'd go to the pound and get one. The dogs would learn to leave it alone, and I could remember how this felt with Jane. A shadow of what this felt like.

Rain fell, but more softly now. "Will this much rain make the conditions dangerous at the Horse Trials?"

"I don't think so. Everything should dry up by then. The rain is already letting up."

I said, "Tell me about your most recent past lover. Didn't you have a girlfriend when you came west?"

"Yes, but I ended it right before then. I was so drawn to her at first. She was a witty, clever conversationalist."

"So, what went wrong?"

"I realized she never said anything kind about anyone."

"Why do you think she was attracted to you?"

"Money. She was such a social climber. I think she liked the fact I come from old money, that I live in an historic home, that sort of thing. She loved art and beautiful things, was a dealer. I thought, mistakenly, that she would be sensitive and cherish life and nature. But I never met a colder person."

"Colder than Georgia?"

Jane smiled. "I think they were made for each other. Your turn."

I was silent, remembering, until Jane poked me in the ribs.

"You know about Hannah. I thought it was the real thing, but way before her, I met this gal, Ginny, at college. We were both in the Ag program and competed in the College Rodeo. Her heroine was Fox Hastings, one of the first women bulldoggers."

"As opposed to bull daggers?" Jane had a mischievous grin. At my puzzled look, she said, "That's what they used to call butches back in the fifties."

"Ha! No kidding. I missed that one. No, this is where a

horned steer is let out of a chute, and you ride out on the left of it with your hazing partner on the right. You slide off your horse, grab the steer's horns, and throw him to the ground."

"Throw him to the ground?" Jane repeated.

"Yeah. Bill Pickett, a black cowboy, was the first. He bit the nose of the steer to throw it. I've always had trouble imagining that one. But that's what they say."

"So, did you ever do this?"

"Bite?" I said, playing with Jane. At her headshake, I answered, "Why, we both did. Even though Ginny was a little smaller than me her timing was better, so she threw them faster."

"Go on. You were telling me about Ginny and you."

"For us, college during the winter felt like a vacation from all the work at home. But here we were in college learning how to do more of it: pregnancy testing cows, artificial insemination, and crop analysis. Ginny's family ran purebred Black Angus on a big ranch west of Augusta. That's under the east slope of the Rocky Mountain front. Beautiful grassland. Her parents also had an outfitter's license for the Scapegoat and Bob Marshall Wilderness areas, and she'd work for them during the summer and during hunting season on some trips. My, those summers were long."

"Couldn't you work for them? Be together?"

"I rode with them helping out on some rides into the Bob, but most of the time, I had to help out my folks. My older brother had left home, and it was just me and Norburt to do the work. My dad could drive the tractor, but not much else since his heart attack. Mom never did any jobs that weren't close to the house."

"So, get back to Ginny."

"We were head over heels in love. She was a swell gal." I ground to a halt, staring at the cold fireplace.

"What happened? Did she leave you for another girl? Come on, this is true confessions time."

"Yeah, she left me on a trip into the Bob going up White River Pass. She was leading the pack string along a narrow trail. The horses ahead of her must've stirred up some bees. They said her horse bucked, slipped over the side and took her...to the bottom."

"Oh, no, Miles, did she die?"

I gave a tight nod. "They had to shoot the horse. Ten years ago. Doesn't get any easier."

"I'm sorry I pressed you to talk about it. I'm sorry." She snuggled in against me again.

"A long time ago."

"Not long enough, I expect."

"No."

CHAPTER TWENTY-TWO

The rest of Friday was filled with indolence, lovemaking and gardening. In the afternoon, it actually dried out enough to go back to the big fall chore of burning leaves. Around the time I struck the match, I thought about having told Jane about Ginny. I'd never said it aloud until then. Never told anyone. A small, tight place in my heart had eased by the act of talking about her. I'd never thought I could love anyone again. I suppose Jane had snuck up on me. I hadn't gone looking, that was for sure.

I'd had more than a few girlfriends since Ginny, but they were too easily left when they became a nuisance. I had to admit that they started annoying me when they wanted to bring more than a toothbrush to the ranch.

I knew someplace around my rib cage was a heart barrier, a fortress of sorts. It wasn't very effective anymore. Either I'd dropped the bridge over the moat, or else Jane had scaled the walls.

I'd swing between open, jelly guts, wanting her in my life always, to a strange, cold realism that to be together, to live together was not going to happen. We were too different and too settled in our differences. We had real impediments. Norburt, for one. I could not leave him on his own. And my life as a rancher was as ingrained in my psyche as herding is to a border collie. I wasn't about to give that up, sell the ranch and move East. And Jane could no more leave her home and life behind than I. Meeting had been a total fluke. Soon it would all become nebulous again. Who would come visit and when? For how long? And then the long periods of time in between that felt like my life was on hold, waiting.

My back ached from all the raking. I arched my shoulders and stretched my hands as high as I could reach, then grabbed the rake and fluffed the pile of leaves. The fire had smoldered out while I'd been daydreaming. I dug the little red box of Diamond matches out of my jeans pocket, slid open the drawer, and struck one on the grit. With the help of pieces of newspaper, the leaves ignited, sending their sweet smell of fall into the air.

I shook my head. God! Cheer up. Having Jane was better than nothing. Deep inside, a small voice said, "Oh, yeah?" Would it just end up with more heartache? Living in that limbo of myth that a relationship existed in spite of spending most of the time alone?

Jane slipped her arms around me from behind. "Where did you go?" she asked.

"Thinking about the last bit of time left us. Two days and three nights." I smiled at her, intoning in a deep movie announcer voice, "Will we use it wisely?"

"I dearly hope so." She rose to her toes and kissed me long and soft.

"We could start now," I whispered in her ear.

"Is there something about burning leaves that turns you on?" Jane took the rake from my hands and leaned it against the stone garden wall.

"Maybe," I said with a drawl, fake cowboy-like. "Maybe it's because there are so few at home, and the ones from the cottonwoods and aspens are ripped off the trees by the wind and taken to Billings or Fargo. Sometimes you'll find a dune of them against a log or something. Raking is an act of futility."

"Oh, come on." Jane grabbed the hose, sprayed out the fire, and then led me into the house.

I didn't resist. Passion overtook me around the third kiss, which came galloping up when I unsnapped Jane's bra and let her breasts free. I gently lifted one of them to feel the weight, the suppleness. Brought my lips to the hard nipple and lightly touched it with my tongue. I slid my hand down her back to that small hollow above the round of her buttocks. I unbuttoned her jeans, then pulled her hips against my body and held her tight with a hand cupping each round side of her rump. I pushed her back on the bed and pulled her jeans all the way off.

The ache in me burned. Maybe she was right about that leaves thing.

❖

We set the alarm for four o'clock the next morning. We'd made our own plans for Quail Mountain in eastern Massachusetts. Jane would groom for Vic, so she needed to leave by five, and we had packed the car earlier.

Vic rode at the lowliest Novice level, which took the course first. Naomi tested at the uppermost, Grand Prix level, which came last.

I had called Naomi to ask if I could catch a ride in her classy red Jeep. She agreed and said she'd pick me up at the barn; she just needed to make sure Milk was ready to travel. The new working student often got to the barn late, and Naomi liked to put the leg wraps on herself.

Jane would drop me off at North Winds Farm, go pick up

Vic, and drive to Quail Mountain. We knew Nancy, a working student hired since Arthur's death, would drive the horse van. In an act of largesse, Georgia had given everyone else in the barn the day off, mentioning a side trip to Newfane to drop off tack for repair. She planned to arrive at the event grounds in time for Victoria's test.

❖

The alarm had a brain-piercing high beep that left me feeling that an alien had struck. The aroma of brewing coffee called to me. Jane was still curled up against me, so she had set the timer on the pot before going to bed. I kept my eyes tightly closed while I listened to the sounds of Jane rising, going to the kitchen, opening the cabinet doors. I found myself imprinting my memory with segments of Jane. Filed for future reference. The coffee delivery arrived, Jane plumping my pillows and placing the warm mug in my hands. "Ah. Good coffee." I closed my eyes and breathed out. "Makes getting up at four almost tolerable."

"I'll make another batch to fill a go cup for you."

"Heaven."

"Do you want anything to eat? We could pick up a doughnut."

"Sugar first thing? Sends my nervous system into a tailspin. I'll fry some bacon." My feet hit the floor.

"Nothing for me."

I stopped in the bedroom doorway and turned to watch her dress. "Not even scrambled eggs?"

"You're such a voyeur."

"You bet. Eggs?"

"Okay. One."

"How do you scramble one egg? Oh, I'll figure out something."

The bacon sizzled. Bright orange juice sat in two glasses on the little table by the kitchen window, framing dark night. Jane came into the kitchen. She watched me place the bacon on a paper towel. "Seems strange to be setting out breakfast in the dark."

"Not to me. I'm always up before the sun."

Jane held back on the bacon, but did lay on some scrambled eggs, toast, and the juice. I cleaned my plate, wiping it up with a piece of toast.

The day would be long, and if the girls' school was any indication of food at Horse Trials, Quail Mountain would be the same. Concession stands were just too tacky, don't you know? At the worst scenario, I'd take one of the cars to the nearest town to pick up some lunch. A hoagie, as they called subs out here.

Jane slipped her arm around me, and I was transported back to Putney. "I've been thinking, or maybe it's feeling," she said. "I love you. More than I thought possible or ever loved anyone, and the idea of your leaving is making me hurt. I can't imagine what it will be like after you're gone. I tried to 'busy' myself so I wouldn't feel the loss of you this last summer, then I got caught up in Georgia's mess. I don't think I can do it again."

I turned and fully held her. "Yes, well, it is a stumper, what to do with this relationship."

"I've decided to put the house in the hands of an estate agent to rent. I'd like to bring Moonglow and Dusty and, of course, Scout. Do you think you can stand it? This huge addition to your family?"

I was stunned. She had been struggling with the same

issues I had and come up with a plan. "You mean actually live together?" I tried to keep the rush of panic out of my eyes. The idea would grow on me. The trouble was I had already begun the process of separation and would need to regroup.

"Yes. I could get everything in storage, shipping arranged, and arrive there by Christmas." Jane's warm brown eyes were shiny, brighter than usual from tears about to slip over the lower lashes. "This is something you want, too, isn't it? The upstairs of the farmhouse is unused, so I can set up a writing space in one of those old bedrooms. The lack of Internet access is a problem. Maybe I'll write that novel I've always wanted to."

"You won't change your mind? If I get back and start dreaming you there, it will all come true? I'll wake up one morning to you beside me, your clothes in the closet and Norburt saying 'good morning, Miz Scott.' I won't tell Burt until you're actually on your way."

"You're scared, aren't you, Miles?" Jane's gaze had turned questioning.

Mixed in with the sudden prospect of change rose a deep excitement laced with hope that this woman I loved would actually be living with me. I had so thoroughly excluded sharing a home with her that I had forgotten how to imagine us together in all those small ways: reading in the evenings, watching the Northern Lights, riding to check on the cows.

"The truth is I've never lived with a lover, except that disastrously stifling time with Hannah. So, I guess, yes. I am scared as hell. But the alternative is bleak." I took in a long, slow breath. "Time I learned, wouldn't you say?"

CHAPTER TWENTY-THREE

One thing I was sure of, I'd never gone to any horse event in daylight. But I was surprised that the barn was dark. I knew I was a little earlier than Naomi and I had agreed on, but I thought someone would be busy at the barn. I slipped out of Jane's car. The whir of her electric window going down brought me to her side. "Give me a kiss," she whispered.

I stuck my head through the window, into the warmth of her car, her breath. "See you soon, darling." I licked her ear.

Jane gave a soft scream and pushed me aside. She put her car in gear and drove away. I stood there watching her car lights vanish, then turned toward the barn. All the lights were off at both the barn and Georgia's house up on the hill. The horse van, with side ramp down and ready, waited near the main door. So, I was early. The gravel in the driveway crunched louder in the dark than during the day. A gust of predawn wind moaned in the trees. Naomi and her red Jeep weren't in sight yet, and it didn't look like the working student had risen to shine. She had an apartment in Putney, as Arthur's digs weren't cleaned out yet.

I figured Georgia had already left on her side trip to Amherst or was still asleep.

I figured wrong. I entered the dark barn trying to remember

where the light switch was located. Something hit me so hard, I simply lay on the ground with a feeble effort at wondering how I got there. Rough hands grabbed one of my arms, rolled me on my back, and I felt plastic handcuffs pulled tighter than necessary around my wrist. The other wrist was similarly handled then linked together by a third plastic strap.

Somebody dragged me down the clay floor, my heels feeling like they left a trail of my body parts, like Hansel's crumbs. I heard a heavy stall door slide open. I was rolled, kicked, and otherwise unceremoniously gotten into the stall, which wasn't clean. I smelled the pungent aroma of manure near my face, and I groaned weakly. The person took another strip of plastic and fed it through the axle of what I later discovered was Arthur's fated wheelbarrow, linking my arms in front of me.

I gasped for breath, mouth wide open, the pain from the rib kicks forcing me into short, careful pants. I could taste the saddle soap from a tack cleaning sponge shoved into my mouth. Georgia's silver bracelets tinkled as she wrapped a leg bandage around my head, over one eye and the sponge. Once I was safely trussed, she kicked me with a viciousness that scared the hell out of me.

She never said a word to me. She didn't have to warn me to lie still. I was hurting so bad that wasn't a problem. She threw some straw over me and slid the door closed, bolting the latch.

Lights flashed on and I heard the scratch of the rake, no doubt covering the marks my body had left in the dirt aisle. She must be raking the long chevron pattern that Arthur had elevated to a fine art.

Georgia climbed the ladder to the hayloft to feed the horses. Dropping hay into the corner feeders through the trap doors made short work of quieting the equine demands. A car engine died near the front door. I heard Georgia's shrill voice, "I said five o'clock, Nancy. It's about time you got here. Five thirty is not five o'clock. What do you think this is? A country club?"

Nancy responded with an element of annoyance. "I distinctly heard you say five thirty."

"Don't argue with me!"

I grunted, shifting to a more comfortable position. No, I didn't imagine this was Georgia's Resort. My brain functioned at a slow speed, but it came to me that Georgia had purposely misled Nancy about the time. She had planned to incapacitate and jail me, and I didn't like to think about why she was doing this.

"No time to clean stalls. I've already fed," Georgia said.

Another car engine died, then a door slammed. Probably Naomi. I heard my name faintly, with Georgia's response a brisk "Not coming. Sick, I think." All the sounds of people talking and car doors slamming seemed to be offstage. As a player, this wasn't my scene.

I heard the footfalls of two horses being led down the far parallel aisle, and sounds from the tack room next to the main door told me they were loading the van. The big front spotlights were lit. Inside the stall, gray reflected light filtered through the high window.

Naomi said, "If you're sure Miles won't be coming, then I'll go on ahead."

"No! I already told…" Georgia lowered her voice from the upper shrieking registers. "She's sick."

You're the one who's sick, I thought. *And, girl, you are wound tight enough to snap.* They'd all leave soon. I had to get free. I didn't know what Georgia was saving me for, but it wasn't going to be pretty. Even more, I worried what she had up her sleeve for Jane. I banged my feet against the wall, trying to draw someone other than Georgia's attention.

"Get on with it," I heard Georgia say. "That's just Money's Worth acting up. I'll turn him out as soon as you leave."

The sound of Nancy shifting through the gears of the van galvanized me to my knees. I was too late. I heard Georgia's footsteps coming toward me. Our eyes made contact through the bars. "You, I'll deal with later. Hope you're comfy."

I heard the click of a padlock on the door slide, and fell back to the straw.

I had no way to break out of this prison. She knew it. I knew it. I lay back and scanned the walls. My only hope was that someone would stumble into the barn and find me here. First thing, then, was to get this gag off. Animals are helpless lying down, and most will struggle to their feet if threatened. The same instinct drove me. If there was a way, I had to get up and out of here before Georgia came back and finished the job.

Once again I rolled to my knees, waiting a moment until my head quit spinning. The leg bandage holding the tack sponge in my mouth came off fairly easily when I rubbed my head against the wheelbarrow. The Velcro worked loose and the whole business unraveled. I spat the sponge out on the straw and worked my tongue past my soapy teeth, spitting a few times.

Oh, what I wouldn't give for a mouthful of water.

When I reached my feet, I hunched over my stomach, grunting like an old sow. My tender midriff had caught a solid punch. Slow, shallow breaths were the best I could do. I shook ineffectively, knocking some of the straw off. With one hand, I got the wheelbarrow tilted up against the handlebars, allowing me to get more vertical. If I chose to accept it. My head spun, and it felt like a knife was sticking into my brain, right between my eyes. I waited as still as possible for the pain to ebb.

I yearned for my pearl-handled pocketknife back in Helena. I looked all around the inside of the stall for something protruding or sharp. But this place was a classy facility and nothing of that sort would be allowed. The stall looked even more like a jail from the inside. Mentally I went through my pockets. My wallet was inaccessible in my hip pocket. What did I think, anyway? That I could bribe one of the horses to let me go? They eyed me with suspicious, quick glances. I was not quite an intruder, but not where I belonged either.

Okay, not the wallet. Rubbing the outside of my pockets, I counted a couple of used snot rags. And a strange lump in one front pocket. Not much. What was the lump? A wad of dollar bills? I'd have to work it up out of my pants even to know. It came to me in a flash. Jane and I had burned leaves and I had one of the small Diamond matchboxes. I wondered what the matches would do to the plastic cuffs. Seemed like the only show in town.

Pretzel woman at the Lewis and Clark Fair had nothing on me. Getting close to that little box of wooden matches snuggled next to my crotch was like an elusive courtship. I felt the sandy strike area with one fingertip, and then the box shyly turned away. My hands were as ungainly as mating octopods.

I lay back down on the tarnished straw and got cozy with the wheelbarrow. This wheelbarrow had served a sinister use for Georgia once before. I was damned if it would again.

I managed to work the box north to the slit at the top of my pocket. Catching it with two scissor fingers, I drew the prize out from the denim shelter. I dropped it in some especially wet manure. Had to pick it up with my teeth.

CHAPTER TWENTY-FOUR

My hands appeared helpless and far away. I wiggled my body closer to them with the manure-spotted box in my teeth, lips snarling back. I felt like a retrieving dog passing the prize to her master's hand. With an odd detachment, I watched the fingers clutch the green and red box. Blue print declared them Diamond and beneath that, white lettering on a blue banner read, *Strike On Box Matches*.

Oh, great. Not *Strike Anywhere Matches*. Like back in my cool and callow youth, when I would light a girl's cigarette by sweeping the match on my blue jeans, from butt along thigh, presenting the lit match as magic. I didn't have a lot of sweeping room right now. If I got one little red-headed sucker lit, it would be a miracle.

Using my teeth, I managed to pull the crunched match drawer out. The little green-tipped rescuers waited for me to select one of them without spilling the box. I managed to pick up three with thick unresponsive fingers, deadened by the lack of circulation. This was a good thing. I didn't spill the rest of them.

I pushed the drawer closed again. With my teeth and one set of fingers, I braced the box against the wheelbarrow in order to strike against it. A torch flared up, and I maneuvered it under a plastic strap. The melting plastic ran down against my wrist and stuck to my skin. I howled and dropped the match. At least now my hands were separate, the connecting plastic burned away.

Sweat trickled down my back like ants between my shoulder blades. I wiped my forehead against my shoulder while I kneed out the tiny golden flames in the straw. Great way to solve my problems, burn the barn down. A rustle of nervous horses moving through bedding reminded me that I wouldn't be the only crispy critter. Grunting out the waves of pain, I waited for it to back off.

The second time around, I'd lost my innocence. My hands were shaking so bad I could hardly light the match. Without blood circulating, my fingers were growing unresponsive, and I fumbled the lit match to the straw. This time I threw my whole body down over the tiny flame.

As I lay there, an odd flash came to mind of myself as a kid playing with matches in the barn. I'd only done this once, discovering at an early age that too much was at stake. I remember how sweat was running down every inch of me before I got the flames out. Hiding the burnt straw evidence was another chore. After this, I played out in the sagebrush, lighting little "campfires." Once one of them went wild, and I had to get help to stamp it out. I thought I'd learned my lesson, but here I was again playing with matches.

The soft straw held me in comfort, seductively wanting me to lie there, passively. To do nothing, because to move made everything hurt. I took in a long slow breath of air. Georgia no longer had anything that regulated her. She was out of control and believed she was invincible. I tried to sort out what her motives were for killing Megan. Killing her father was horrific. Understandable, but nonetheless horrific. And surely I was on the "to-do" list. Motives usually went: one, money and two, love. How weird. Love as a motive to kill. Three, a secret. Somewhere in the mix was revenge.

My guess was that she'd murdered her mother for money with a strong dose of revenge, her father for revenge and keeping the humiliating secret, as well as covering Megan's death and the switch of horses. Amazing he'd lived that long. I thought all three applied to Megan. Of all of them, I thought the secret of her homosexuality the most likely, and the deepest underlying motive. And now it was anyone who stood in her way. How could she ever think that once she got rid of me, everything would go back to normal?

What drove me now was the clear likelihood that she would try to kill Jane. Thinking about Jane galvanized me to get back to my odious job. My fingertips had turned blue. For the third time, I went through the match routine. When the green head flared up, I put it straight to the plastic joining my wrists. Sweat ran down my face in rivers. The sounds that came out of my mouth had no relation to the human animal.

The plastic band gave way, and I fell back to the straw. Deep breaths helped empty the pain from my body on each exhale. Every breath had a little whine at the end of the air. I flung my free arm out to one side, resting it palm up. At least one hand was free of the strangling circle of plastic. Needles seemed to prick my hand in a million places as the blood flooded back into the starved fingers. I made a fist and then stretched my fingers out, pumping blood into my hand.

My flannel long-sleeved shirt was soaking wet, especially where I wiped my face. A long glacial shudder racked me as the sweat cooled. I had more to do, but not yet. I wasn't ready to go to stage two. That disembodied hand felt like electric spiders danced across the palm and down my fingers. I kept opening and closing my hand, trying to help pump the blood back to all the little capillaries that were screaming for circulation.

The second hand was much easier to free. Grasping the seared end of the plastic strap in my teeth, I could get it away from my skin. A fraction, but enough to make the experience something I could handle. I rubbed that wrist where a deep groove circled. A blister was already forming from the burn. I couldn't touch or look at the other one.

I figured I had one advantage now, at least. When Georgia returned, I could fake that I was still restrained and jump her. I leaned against the wall of the stall and stared at the window. The light had changed to bright daylight. To hell with waiting for Georgia to return. She wouldn't come for me until after Jane was dead. Time passed at warp speed, and I had to get to Jane.

Georgia had closed and latched both sections of the stall door, and I was sure I'd heard the click of a padlock. No bars were on that section. It was all solid wood, so I couldn't reach through to the bolt. I got close to the bars along the front to try to see the bolt latches. They were definitely out of reach, and I could see the rounded edge of the padlock. I paced the length of each twelve-foot wall. The stall on one side had a horse who laid his ears back at me. I told him, "Don't worry, I can't get into your stall. Your food is safe from me."

I suppose a silly part of me hoped someone had left a rake or pitchfork where I could reach it. Or I'd find a rope coiled, hanging handy so I could loop it over something. Or that someone might arrive for a morning ride. That would be so easy, but I could not wait on the slim possibility that would happen. I placed one hand over my ribs where Georgia had landed the most vicious kick. I didn't think they were broken, just very sore. I tested out my range of motion by raising my hands above my head, and it was something I could manage.

The walls went all the way to the ceiling, which was the floor of the hayloft. Even if I could climb the bars, I didn't have enough room at the top to squeeze out. I looked up at the ceiling. The hayloft. Above the hayrack was a chute hole with a trap door in the floor. Each group of four stalls had one hole above the metal cage that held the hay. Four horses could be hayed from above, directly into their feeding rack.

I jumped for the top of the rack to swing my feet up, but I hit a wall of pain so intense I let go and fell back to the floor. I rolled over on my back, squeezed my eyes tight, grunted a few times, and thought about a different approach. That old wheelbarrow would be pressed into service again. I parked it right under the rack, climbed in, and managed to step on up. Balancing on the top wrought iron rim, I pushed the chute door open with my head. In the process, I managed to kick over the wheelbarrow from underneath me. I had no choice but to bite the bullet and pull myself up into the hayloft.

I kicked and struggled, inching my way up to the top of the hayrack and through the hole. I rested halfway through, body aching. In the dark hayloft, I tried to get to my feet and simply fell back to the floor. I lay there a few more minutes thinking this must be how climbers felt who have reached the summit of Mt. Everest: exultant, spent, and wondering how the hell they would get back down.

Descent for me would be a challenge as well, I imagined. I had to negotiate the ladder, but my hands were not reliable. I lay there in comfort imagining exactly how I would accomplish my next feat. There was another way. If I could get through Arthur's rooms, I could go out the door and down the side flight of stairs. This idea got me to my feet and to the door into his apartment, which was padlocked. I only threw myself, in frustration, against the door once. I paced across the hayloft floor but couldn't find anything to use to pry the door open. I went to the hay drop doors, opening them as I went down the center of the barn. Hitting a piece of luck, I came to Milk of Kindness's stall. The jail door stood wide open. I did a pretty good Tarzan call of the elephants after I slid through the trap door, grasped the hayrack, and dropped to the straw. Here I am again. This time I got up and walked through the open door. In the tack room, I located a pair of pigskin riding gloves and found Cat's gear. He didn't want to leave his hay, but I saddled him up while he ate. I rode across pastures to the east, not wanting to risk facing Georgia on the roads. Her facility was not far away from the major north-south interstate.

The pastures proved frustrating, as many of them had only one gate. In the West, we always have gates at the corners. The pastures at home are square miles or larger, so to reach a corner and not be able to get out can make travel difficult. Pretty maddening for me, even in these ten-acre fields.

I heard the swish of cars and saw their shiny bodies racing along the pavement of the interstate. I jumped off Cat, unsaddled him, led him into a field, and turned him loose. I hung his tack on the gate and made my way to the south side of the highway.

CHAPTER TWENTY-FIVE

The package I presented thumbing south on the interstate was not an inviting one. I'd tried to rake the straw out of my hair with my fingers and brush most of the manure clumps off my clothes. All the drivers of the really nice cars and SUVs passed me without a glance. Some actually sped up. My mind was busy exploring the possibility of car theft when I heard the screech of brakes.

"Hey! You a real cowgirl? Come on, gal."

The car had more purple bumper stickers and rainbow decals than I'd ever seen before on any one vehicle. The dented, gas-guzzling conveyance was filled with pierced, buck-haired cuties of college age. I gave them my all-time best grin, said, "You bet I am."

The six gals were headed for North Hampton, which I learned was New England Dyke Heaven. They packed me in the midst of them with lots of giggles and sardine jokes.

"Where you from?"

"Montana."

"Ooh. That's real cow country. You have cows?"

"Smells like it." One cute gal pinched her nose.

"Mmm-hmm, and horses," I answered.

"What you doing out here, you handsome cowgirl?"

"Making sure nobody is horning in on my territory. My gal lives in Vermont." I had an intense euphoria, from being free, from being submerged in a car of young dykes.

"Hey, baby, she don't want you, I'm here."

"Yeah, she a fool?"

One purple-haired gal got a look at the burn on my wrist.

"What's this? You into kinky sex?"

Her eyes told me she knew something was wrong, and she was only teasing. I started grinning. They were all so sweet.

"Doesn't this hurt? I can't believe you're just grinning."

"Oh, yeah. But I'm so happy."

"Get this girl some aspirin. Look in the glove compartment!"

"Here, take my water bottle."

"Sal, let me have your scarf."

"What happened?"

While I told them a quick version of what had happened, they tenderly wrapped my bad wrist.

"Oh, baby. This isn't good. That must be some sick bitch."

"Well, actually I did it to myself getting free."

"I meant the tying up part," Purple Hair said with patience.

"We have to take the cowgirl where she want to go."

"I wouldn't mind getting my hands on the twisted bitch who did this to you," Purple Hair said. "Will she be where we're going?"

"I'd like to keep that pleasure for myself," I claimed.

A deep-throated laugh answered. "Oh, oh, baby. She better watch out."

The bold and lively gals came to a sudden hush when we entered the gates of Quail Mountain. The car had a certain stately quality, like a sleek shark, as it negotiated the luxury SUVs and the tank-like Hummers. We pulled into a space on the grassy pasture, parking next to a white-painted four-board fence.

"It's so posh," one of the young women said.

"God! I thought it was just a horse show."

"I don't want to go there," Purple Hair said. "Look at us— torn jeans and overalls?"

"Yeah. We rock, but we might get stoned."

"I wouldn't mind getting stoned," came from one of the gals in the front seat.

Secretly, I was tickled. I wanted to not be noticed. These women remembered their mother's warnings about social norms and behavior.

"Look, this is closer than I ever imagined I'd get," I said, not wanting them to feel obligated to do more.

"You can't go in there with that shit-covered shirt. Is that one of your favorites, or…?"

Each one of them was on the verge of ripping her shirt off and handing it to me.

I grinned my best. "Now how would I look in a Lady Gaga T-shirt? You gals are all wonderful, but I'll be okay in this. I'll move fast so no one can see the stains. I'm not going calling, anyway."

I glanced at the two-hundred-year-old brick manor house of Quail Mountain. The mansion stood on a slight rise, backed by stately oaks. The bright flames of turning maple trees raucously covered the surrounding hills. Rolling green pastures edged with startling white board fences or rock wall enclosures ranged in all directions. Intense areas of activity surrounded the car park, and exhibitors' parking was filled with every imaginable horse transport.

I reached for the door handle, then stopped when I saw all the expectant faces aimed at me. "Give me an address, and I'll tell you all about what happened."

"You have email out there in sagebrush country?" Purple Hair asked.

"Sure do. Once I rig the horse to the treadmill and get the electric geared up."

They were not quite sure if they believed me or not. I kept a straight face and took the little scrap of paper on which Jill had scribbled her email address.

"It was fun." I smiled. "Thanks. You are all the best."

"You take care of yourself." They all had something to say.

"Keep those hands out of the flame."

"Tell that girlfriend of yours to shape up."

"Maybe one of these days we'll drive out to visit you on the ranch."

I could see a small crush taking shape in Purple Hair's eyes.

I nodded and touched my nonexistent hat brim. "You would always be welcome."

The engine coughed to life, sending out a choking cloud of black exhaust.

CHAPTER TWENTY-SIX

The first thing I had to do was find Jane, and Victoria would know where to find her. Victoria shouldn't be too hard to locate with the black mare under her. I did not want to come upon Georgia unawares. I drew some suspicious stares as I slowly moved through the car park area toward the exhibitors' parking. Large, fancy horse vans and trailers covered a fifty-acre field.

While lurking behind a large maroon horse van with living quarters, I spotted the white horse with Naomi. Georgia stood by the van. A third person, the groom, gave Naomi a leg up into the saddle and ran a white buffing cloth over her boots and the shining silver stirrups. Georgia handed Naomi a black top hat then stood back, giving her directions. Naomi drew on white gloves, nodded to Georgia, and rode away to warm her horse up before the dressage test.

I watched for a few more moments, not seeing either Jane or Vic and Night. I backed up into somebody standing behind me and about jumped out of my skin.

"I say, what are you doing here?" demanded a tweedy, well-fed man holding a snarling Jack Russell terrier.

"Looking for a friend riding Novice," I answered as boldly as possible.

"Over there." He waved, flicking his fingertips. "Finishing the cross-country portion."

"Thank you so much," I said, beating a hasty retreat lest he put the terrier to ground.

The direction was opposite Georgia, so I was happy. I came to a place where brightly dressed riders circled their snorting, pulling horses, ready to ride one by one through a set of poles forming a timing gate. Riders wore vivid colors in this phase of the event. They looked more like race jockeys. A white number bib covered their whole chest and back, way larger than the discreet round number pinned to the bridle and breastplate of the horse for dressage.

A group of people, each one with a task, stood guard at the timing poles. Each horse had to go through the in gate at the start and the out gate to end the course. Someone yelled, "Number forty-three on deck." A woman made notes on a clipboard while a man watched a stopwatch with his hand held high. When he dropped it, number forty-three dutifully shot between the poles, riding uphill to the first jump, a simple three-log oxer. A number to the right of the jump told us Number One. The powerful horse galloped at a steady pace.

The horses would face between eleven and twenty obstacles: water hazards, banks with sheer drops, and double barriers three to four feet high made with logs or stone. Any refusals would take points off the starting score. And a horse that crossed his own tracks or went down was eliminated, as was a rider who fell off anywhere from start gate to finish.

A short distance to the right, horses finishing the course arrived, their heads low, sweat sleeking their necks and white foam making a stripe where the reins slid on each side. They came down to a walk as soon as they cleared the poles, someone calling out their number and noting the time. The rider rode a short distance, slid off, and a groom tossed a cooling sheet over the horse and led the animal away. In a short time they were expected to jump a course in the stadium without a refusal or knocking a jump, doing it with style.

At that moment, I saw a familiar horse and rider approaching the gate at a slow gallop. They came through the poles and stopped, Night looking very fit and strong. Victoria leaned over to say something to the judges. I walked toward them, waving, and Vic looked up, surprised to see me. She gave a nod to the exit judges and then walked Night over to me. "I was eliminated. My stupidity. I simply didn't see jump number seven. Night was going so great, too. What are you doing here? Thought you were sick. Georgia said Jane went home to nurse you."

This sent a chill down my back. I leaned against the black mare and told her what Georgia had done to me back at the barn.

Vic's face paled. "She's done something to Jane." She stated this as fact, not speculation.

"Yes, I'm afraid Georgia has Jane tied up somewhere, too. We're the only ones who know what she's done." I told her about the tan envelope filled with damming evidence.

"If something happens to me, you've got to expose her. This woman is dangerous. Where do you think Jane might be?"

"Miles, she was here at the end of my dressage test." Her face became frozen in memory, and I knew it was something awful. "We were all of us heading out to walk the course together, but Georgia and Jane set off while I waited for Naomi to put her hiking boots on. We planned to meet up at the fourth jump. Georgia was waiting there, but Jane wasn't with her. That's when she told me Jane had gotten a call from you."

We did one of those locked gaze things. I said, "She's somewhere between the start and the fourth jump."

Vic nodded. "Take Night."

"Georgia is by the van finishing up with Naomi. If you can, head her off from going toward the jumps. Don't let on you suspect anything. If she hurt Jane, I'll do some serious damage to her."

Victoria jumped to the ground. "Take my helmet and number. You'll be less noticeable on the course."

The blue and black silk-covered helmet was perfect. I buckled the chinstrap. My cowboy boots and blue jeans did look a mite out of place, but maybe at first glance I'd blend in. The bib covered the disreputable shirt.

"The Advanced course will be set up in a few minutes, when the last horse is off the course. That should give you a space of time without a lot of action. Find her." Vic gave me a boost, and I settled into the saddle.

I let the stirrups out three notches, gathered up the reins, and set off at a good strong trot. I ignored the raised voice and the shouts that followed as I passed the gate.

Night loped up the hill and I gave the first jump a wide berth. I would find Jane later, in a more sheltered and secluded place.

CHAPTER TWENTY-SEVEN

The mare felt good beneath me. We knew each other. She trusted me, and I had grown to trust her, too. I flashed back on the Hell Bitch she had been when I first met her. This mare I rode was a whole different horse: supple, alert, and willing. Her summer vacation in Montana and her life with Vic must have been just what the veterinarian ordered. And in a way, it was.

I hoped I would find Jane strolling between jumps or idly talking with a spectator. I tried to keep my imagination away from the darkest places and not envision Jane suffering the casual cruelty Georgia had dished out to me.

I scanned everything around me. This first part of the course was open, the jumps set in a field. The trees and brush began at the third jump, and here I got off and walked around. It was a broad water jump with a short bank on the leading edge. I heard the sound of galloping hooves.

A voice right behind me yelled, "Get out of the way, you fool."

I spun around and saw a woman with a clipboard in a lawn chair. Ah, I forgot there would be a fence judge, someone to witness whether or not a rider and horse jumped or refused. Her focus would be absolutely on the contestant, though. When this rider passed, I'd ask her if she'd seen anything. Friendly was not an adjective I would use on her. She told me to get out of her penalty zone, whatever that was. I gave up on her in a hurry and rode on toward number four.

Jump number four was a bank jump, a pile of dirt with a jump at the top and a long drop on the far landing. A fence judge sat off to one side on a director's chair. The jump was very exposed, and I couldn't imagine a place where Jane could be hidden. I was on the verge of riding over to him when I realized with a rush that the track ran past the car park. It lay isolated off to the side, surrounded by a dense line of trees. The glint of metal cars shimmered through the branches. I pointed Night in that direction.

The owners' and competitors' parking covered a five-acre field of brightly colored and very expensive cars. Most everyone had parked by this time, leaving for the action at ringside. The deserted parking area had a spooky feel, like the cars were plotting a revolt.

From the vantage point of my tall horse, I could see the roof of Georgia's distinctive Pagoda 280 SL Mercedes parked in the middle of the pack. I rode toward it at a trot calling for Jane. When I reached the car, I jumped off Night to look inside it. It was locked, but I could see nothing. No one on the tiny back boot covered with a blanket. I pounded the roof in frustration.

And heard a muffled sound. A thumping. I spun around and slapped the trunk. "Are you in there, Jane?"

She must have been gagged, but it was Jane all right. She was flipping around like a beached fish. I leaned close and said, "Be still. I'll get you out of there."

I checked all the doors again. Locked up tight, and not one window open even a crack. There must be a trunk release inside. I ran my hands over the hot metal of the trunk lid and explored the smooth edge where I might put a pry bar. The designers had invested some thought into foiling a B&E. I needed to find a substantial piece of iron to get this open.

I was afraid to leave the car in case Georgia came back, but I had to find something to get the trunk open. I patted the lid, bent over, and said, "I'll be back in a jiffy." I stepped on the bumper and got back on Night. The only person in sight was the fence judge. I rode over to him. I explained that I needed a tool, a pry bar.

"What for?" His eyes were hard with suspicion.

"A friend of mine is locked in the trunk of a car—"

He picked up a radio with a long antenna and pushed a side button. I thought he was calling for help. He said, "I have a very strange person here who wants help breaking into a car. She's riding a black horse—"

I didn't wait to hear anymore. I couldn't go back to the farm hosting the event. I was a marked woman, riding a notable horse. I had to find some other way to get the trunk open. I'd just kick the damned window in. Let anyone try and stop me. I turned Night around and rode back to the car park.

After I tied the mare to a tree, I ran over to the lovely old car and proceeded to climb on the hood and kick to the side to break the window. Nothing happened. I needed to find a hefty rock, so I searched the edge of the parking area. I found one about the size of a cat and returned at a run to the car.

As I raised my arms to slam it into the glass, someone grabbed me at the elbow and spun me to the ground. While I was down and stunned, I watched Georgia slide her key into the lock and enter the car. As I lunged to my feet, she shoved the car into reverse and took off.

I shook my head to clear it, then ran to Night and vaulted on. I was so grateful that Vic had gone off-course and been eliminated so that Night was fresh. The mare had also been in the West at higher altitude and had gotten fit doing some work. Real work. Night took off like a black bullet, catching up with the Mercedes before Georgia could get through the exit gate. Georgia left the track and drove out over the cross-country course. At a jump, she had to slow down to maneuver around the jump sandwiched in between rocks and trees.

This action brought the fence judge out of her chair and on course, screaming and waving her arms. She stopped and frantically fiddled with her two-way radio. Then I rode past, and that put her over the top. "You can't be doing this!" she yelled.

By now we had attracted quite a following.

A competing rider had made the third jump. She was now coming at a steady gallop uphill toward us. Georgia was driving recklessly, and the rider was looking down. I prayed they wouldn't collide.

Maybe it was the sound of the engine, out of place in that jump course setting, that made the rider look up. I saw stark terror etched there. At the last possible moment, Georgia turned out of the way. Glancing over my shoulder, I was amazed to see the rider had gotten her horse over the jump and was heading for the next obstacle. A blue ribbon horse, for sure. And rider.

Georgia was past caring about exposure. Her operating gear was desperation. My forehead felt chilled, even in the sun. A cool breeze worked at my fear-sweat. Was there any way to stop her? Georgia changed direction and drove away from the buildings and the thick of action, toward the end of the jump course. I didn't know for sure, but guessed she knew another way out to a main road.

I had to catch her, or Jane would be dead. I gave Night a rude kick to the ribs, and she gave a little buck but put the speed on. My mind raced over the possibilities as Night narrowed the distance. The window on the driver's side was rolled down because I could see Georgia's elbow, jabbing out the window as she jerked the car around.

I could jump on the car, like the heroes of old stagecoach-runaway horses in the movies. Not much to grab on to considering the sleek design of the Mercedes. I'd probably slip right off the back. We closed fast, and I still hadn't worked out a plan that could see print in anything other than comic books. Fortunately, the pastures were uneven and rough enough that Georgia couldn't floor the gas pedal. The sports car bounced high, leaving the ground and slamming down, tires tearing at the grass.

Nothing slowed the mare. Her steel shoes dug into the uneven ground, eating up the distance. We drew alongside and I shouted at her, "Pull over. There's no way—"

Her laughter was like glass breaking. If I could grab the keys and yank them out of the ignition, that would stop her. I remembered some car-crazed guy telling me that in the early models you could actually remove the key while the car was in operation.

Bulldogging. Now that might be a way to go. The car's low-slung frame meant I'd be diving down, just like reaching for a steer's horns. I kicked my stirrups free, leaned low to the side of the saddle, grabbed both sides of the open window frame, and slipped from the horse. In one smooth move, I dove between Georgia's chest and the steering wheel, got the keys, turned them, and they came away in my hand. Holding them in a tight fist, I let myself slide back out the window.

I landed pretty hard, but not as hard as Georgia. The Mercedes plowed into a stone wall, crunching the luxury car so that it was ready for a metal recycling yard. Night veered to one side, came to a straddle-legged halt, and watched me writhe on the ground, all the old injuries renewed. Georgia frantically worked the door handle, couldn't get it open, and crawled out the window. She stood with one hand splayed out on the hood of the car, moaning. "You've wrecked my car! It's ruined. My beautiful car." She staggered a bit and then climbed the stone wall to run along the far side.

Right then I didn't give a damn about her or her fucking car. I leaped up and went to the trunk. "Honey, are you okay? I'm right here. Get you out in a jiffy."

Where was the damn release? I didn't hear any answering thumps.

My scalp felt like it would blow off my head. "Jane, give me some sign you're all right."

CHAPTER TWENTY-EIGHT

I heard the sound of horse hooves coming fast, then a calm voice say from behind me, "You have to use the trunk key."

I spun around and saw a woman, gray hair in a bun, sitting on a tall chestnut horse.

"Oh. Right," I said, somewhat stupidly, and found the keys still gripped in my fist. I fumbled through them, trying one after the other, until one slid in and turned the trunk lock. The lid swung up, exposing Jane curled up in the cramped space. An empty hypodermic syringe lay beside her. I picked it up, feeling my body grow cold, then tossed it to one side.

As I reached for her, a brown bottle about an inch long rolled away. It had a rubber top and a white and red label. I put my arms beneath her, but she was so limp she was hard to lift, just slid out of my grasp. I hauled her out with the help of the gray-haired woman, and we stretched Jane out on the grass.

Next to me, the woman said into a walkie-talkie, "We need some medical attention. Bring the ambulance up to the gate between jumps twelve and nineteen."

I removed the gag and saw Jane's blue lips. I felt for a pulse but couldn't find one at her neck or wrist. "No!"

I breathed in her mouth to get her lungs filled, and heard the sigh of air coming out, without being followed by an intake.

"Breathe!" Somewhere I'd learned hearing was the last to go. Her hands and feet were bound with the same plastic cuffs Georgia had used on me. Jane's fingertips were blue. A knife appeared just as I was trying to figure out what to do. The gray-haired woman held it out to me. It was a pearl-handled one. I got the blade flat under one of the straps and easily slipped the knife through the plastic. Jane's arm fell limply to one side. I went back to inflating her lungs. After the first few breaths, I felt a hand on my shoulder.

"Let me give it a try." A woman in an EMT jacket put a stethoscope to her chest. I stood to get out of her way, backed up a few steps, and then dropped heavily to one knee. Her partner began a survey. The guy looked at his partner and shook his head. Just once.

"Jane." Her name came out as a moan. She was dead. "She's been drugged."

The EMT woman approached me. "I'm sorry, there was nothing we could do. What did you say? She was drugged, what makes you think—"

With one hand, I waved toward the truck of the car. "It's in there." I looked up at the woman while my lethargic mind pieced it all together. "A drug to destroy horses. The woman who was driving that car…" My voice trailed off to nothing.

This not-me disembodied person watched people around me acting, moving around, taking care of things. They placed the stretcher alongside Jane. The three of them drew her onto it, covering her with a gray blanket.

The EMT woman walked to the trunk of the wrecked car and lifted the syringe, then turned to stare at me. "You think this was used on her?"

"I'm sure of it. It's a drug to euthanize horses. Look at the bottle, it's in there, too."

She dropped the syringe and bottle into a plastic bag.

"Somulose," she read aloud. "Lots of warnings on here for the person administering the drug."

"I can imagine. There's enough in that tiny bottle to kill a large horse." My voice got gravelly.

"This is a crime scene," the EMT woman said to her partner. "We'll have to get the police here and not move her."

I felt a hand grasp my arm, and I saw it was the kind woman who had arrived on the horse.

"The knife," she said.

I looked stupidly at it, open and grasped tightly in my hand. The trouble was, I was holding the business end. Blood seeped from three long slices through the pigskin gloves and across my palm. Staring at it was like listening to a foreign language. My brain couldn't grasp hold of the meaning. I felt no pain.

I wiped the blade on my jeans, folded the knife, and handed it back to her. Urgency pulled at me. The last I'd seen of Georgia was her escape along the stone wall. I could do nothing more here.

"I've got to do something. Tell me where she, where they take her." My throat closed up and that was the last word.

She gave a crisp nod, pointed to the mansion on the hill, and said, "I live there. I've got a call out to the police. Don't leave without stopping in at the house."

CHAPTER TWENTY-NINE

Night grazed a few feet away, unaware of people's major life events. She was just being a horse. I wanted nothing more than to be a horse right then, moving one step to the next bright mouthful bursting in my mouth, its scent rising to my nostrils. One breath, deeper than the rest, filling my chest, springing my ribs, and the slow sigh of the exhale.

Night took one step forward, and magically one of my legs moved forward, too. The reins ran back from the bit, one from each snaffle ring, joined in a small buckle. She had somehow avoided stepping inside the loop followed by throwing up her head, a favorite horse trick.

My focus had dissipated into that of a detached observer. I glanced back over my shoulder to see the ambulance slowly approaching. No urgency there.

Like reassembling parts to the puzzle, I looked around. I saw the lady with the chestnut horse, her eyes directed at me, serious and solemn. The Mercedes, which would never race down the highways again, was now a junkyard dog. A crowd of strangers began gathering, staring, and whispering.

Someone would try to stop me from going after Georgia.

I spun around, took up the mare's reins, and vaulted into the saddle, landing on the leather with a whoosh of pain. The slashes across my palms were real, not remembered. Bloody paw prints on the leather marked where I'd braced my hands for the vault. My grandmother's pioneer voice came to me from the far-off Bozeman Trail: "School in your feeling, girl. Don't ever let them get the upper hand."

Time for me to refocus, to gather every bit of my hunter instincts to find Georgia. The last I'd seen of her, she had climbed the wall and was going uphill on the far side of the fieldstone wall. We found a good spot, and Night sailed over the wall. I didn't land too hard on her back, or out of balance. She came easily down to a trot, and I scanned along the side of the wall down to where the car had crashed. No sign of Georgia.

That sense of being fractured into many small parts had changed, like a film of an explosion in reverse. Now I was a person with one aim in life: finding Georgia. My entire being had condensed down to a missile. Seek. Find. Destroy.

I searched along the wall, Night traveling at a strong trot. The curve of the land dipped down to a small creek, a few maple trees, and a barn with a big open door. As I scanned the countryside for my target, I saw a rider on a big red and white pinto run into the barn, then suddenly appear on the far side galloping uphill away from me. This must be one of the jumps, placed in the dark of the barn, a challenge for a horse to enter a dark place at a gallop and be asked to jump.

Then I saw a figure stand up and dash toward the barn. Georgia disappeared into the dark interior. I rode straight toward the building, watching to make sure she didn't slip out the far side. The thunder of approaching hooves burst from the grove of maple trees along the track. A bay horse galloped toward the barn jump, panting in blasts matching its stride. He slowed to a trot and entered the barn. I waited, but he didn't come out when he should have. Maybe he refused. I heard a shout and rode up fast. The bay came back out the same door with a couple of people running after it shouting. One of them wore a white numbered bib. The other was the fence judge, and Georgia was on the bay.

Georgia hammered the horse's sides, galloping back the way it had come, breathing hard, air drawn into nostrils round with strain. The barn jump lay toward the end of the course. This horse was tired and ready to quit.

Georgia glanced back over her shoulder and caught sight of me. She kicked and slapped the horse for more speed. On the far side of the maple grove, a pasture rolled over a hill bordered by dense maples changing to red and a stone wall with a rail along the top. The bay labored up the hill with his rider flailing at his sides. We were easily closing on her, but I was choosing a less public place to confront her. She shot a look over her shoulder at me, yanked the horse to the left, and gave it a kick to jump the stone wall.

I saw the horse check, assessing this obstacle; then he made a decision and ran out at the last minute. Georgia flew through the air as though she'd decided to take the jump without the horse. She hit the wall and crumpled to the ground. The horse went a few strides and then stood straddle legged, lowered his head, and blew.

Night came to a halt about ten feet from Georgia. I slid off, tied Night's reins behind her ears, and turned her loose to join the other horse. My body cast a shadow across her face, and I saw fear in her eyes.

"You killed her!" My words shot from my mouth like hard rocks.

"Stay away from me!" She squirmed her back up against the stones. Her left hand held her other arm at the elbow, her face distorted in both pain and hatred. Not a pretty mix.

"Don't you understand what I've said? You hateful piece of shit, you killed her."

"You ruined my car. My beautiful little Pagoda." Tears rolled down Georgia's face.

"Jane was a beautiful woman, and you killed her. And all you can think about is your goddamned car?"

"She was going to slander me. Perverted. She was saying terrible things about me."

"Yes, she was queer. And so are you, but you are the damaged, ugly kind."

"You know nothing of the sort."

"Jane told me about that time at camp." I wanted her to know this—think about it all the rest of her life. "She notified your parents that you were engaged in a love affair with another girl. Jane felt terrible about doing that to you, and you never knew. She told me your dark secret of how your father abused you, punishing you for your queerness.

"You may think you're a passing queer, but I reckon there isn't a person in the horse world hasn't guessed by now. And if they haven't, I'll make sure they know. That can eat at you while you're in jail for the rest of your life for murdering Jane, your father, Megan, her horse and, more than likely, your mother."

"I had to kill the horse. The balloon payment was due on the stables." Tears of self-pity coursed down her face. "The parents will keep their children away. Nobody else loves me, nobody."

"Well, they sure as hell won't bring them to the prison for visiting hours."

By now she was full out blubbering. Instead of engaging my sympathy, it made me hate her more. "Why kill Jane?"

"Jane didn't love me! You set her against me."

"Everything isn't about you."

"You can't prove anything. It'll be my word against some Western hick."

"That's what you think. When the residue in that syringe is analyzed, you'll be nailed. And when you're in lockup, every bull dyke in prison will own you."

Georgia rolled to her knees and pushed herself to her feet with one hand. Her right arm hung limp, but in her other hand she had a stone from the wall, raised like a hammer. A rock whooshed past my ear and grazed my temple. I was ready for her and slugged her in the belly. Her arm flew up to her chest, and with her other arm she clutched it tight, hunched protectively with it at her waist. Each blow I landed on her imprinted my pain on her body.

I didn't hear the rider approach. Hands out of nowhere grabbed me. I tried to fight him off, but I'd spent my energy on Georgia. I was thrown to the ground and felt someone's knee in the middle of my back.

"I need some help here." A two-way radio crackled.

Some other people came near. One of them said, "That's my horse. That woman took him. No, that one."

Another voice. "Here comes Ms. Chamberlain."

More hoofbeats at a trot drummed the sod, and then came to a halt.

"I came on this woman beating the crap out of that blond woman."

"Let her up," came the voice of the woman who'd given me her knife.

Instantly the man let me go, then stood.

I couldn't move. My face was buried in the sweet, green grass, wet from my tears. After a minute, I moved my hands under me and lifted myself off the ground. Had to roll over to one elbow. My hands were covered in blood, some of it mine. I rose to my feet, avoided looking at Georgia, removed Vic's helmet, and roughed up my wet sweaty hair.

The woman they called Ms. Chamberlain said to me, "You need to come to my house. Can you ride your horse?"

I looked stupidly at Night, quietly grazing. "She's Victoria's."

"Nevertheless."

Functioning like a poorly manipulated marionette, I managed to buckle the helmet to the D ring on the side of Night's saddle. Everything seemed oddly detached. I moved within a world without a past or a future. Gathering up Night's reins, I turned to watch Ms. Chamberlain and await further instructions. She was giving them to the man who'd held me down.

"Radio John to bring the Jeep to pick up that..." She waved her hand toward Georgia like she was a bag of trash. "Greg, can you stay here until they come for her?"

"Ms. Chamberlain, do you think it's a good idea, going off with her? I think she may become violent."

"No. I'm not worried. Her actions were understandable. That woman is responsible for the death of her friend. Watch her."

This woman who carried such authority gently touched my arm. She said, "Mount up and follow me."

I held the stirrup iron with my left hand, shoved my foot deep to the arch, struggled to mount, and couldn't without using my hands. The damage of the burns, the blade of the knife and contact with Georgia had made them unusable. I led Night up to the stone wall, positioned her, climbed the wall, and threw myself onto her back. She put her ears back and raised and lowered her head a few times.

The reins proved impossible to hold. I dropped them on

the buckle and used my legs to guide her. I glanced at the competitor whose horse Georgia had commandeered and the sweeper, Greg, who had the job of checking the course after the last rider, and they were looking at me as though I were some psycho.

I followed the sorrel horse Ms. Chamberlain rode. When we returned to the crumpled Mercedes, I saw a Jeep. Inside was an officer of the law who left the vehicle as we rode near. Jane was gone. They'd taken her away.

"John, could we all meet at my house? Sort this out?"

John looked at me and said, "This is…?"

A pause followed his question until I realized it was aimed at me.

My voice lay in some forgotten place, dry and useless. With great effort, I managed to say, "Miles. Becky Miles."

Ms. Chamberlain said, "This woman's friend was taken to the hospital. I'm afraid we were too late to help her. She's dead, and the person responsible is being held by one of my men in the next field." She waved in that direction. To me she said, "This is our chief of police, John Curtis. Please spend a moment with us at my house explaining what has occurred."

When the woman said, "she's dead," it felt as though someone had punched me in the guts. I groaned, cleared my throat. "I couldn't get her out of the trunk. If only I'd gotten her out, before." I groaned. "Georgia must have given the shot while I was…" My voice tapered off because I couldn't think. When had she given that lethal shot?

John broke into my mutterings. "We'll get the residue analyzed. The medical people gave it to me."

"Oh, God." I lay down along the horse's mane.

"Come up to the house until we sort this out. Will you be able to ride your horse there?" she asked me, pointing toward the mansion.

I stared stupidly at her, and then nodded.

"We can put your horse in a box. I'll notify the head groom."

None of this was a request. She merely stated what was going to happen with the absolute expectation that we would comply. Perhaps this was a good thing.

Ms. Chamberlain said, "John, they're waiting for you to pick up the responsible party. Take the track through the woods…"

I didn't hear the rest.

On the way to the house, I saw Victoria huffing and panting up the hill. I waved to get her attention, and she stopped, put her hands on her hips, gasping for breath, and waited for us to ride up. "I paced all around the start box, but after the last horse had gone I just struck out and…" Her voice trailed off at a closer look at my face.

"Jane's dead," I croaked. Perhaps if I repeated it enough times, those words would lose their power to cut through to my heart. This time they missed my heart and flew straight to Vic's.

Vic stared at me. "What? Dead?" All the vitality left her face.

I slipped off Night, and we held each other. "I couldn't stop Georgia in time to save Jane."

"No, no." Her sobs racked my body. It felt like we were the same person cut into two parts, she grieving and my half cold as ice.

A strangely detached part of me noticed bloody spots on the back of Vic's blue shirt. I couldn't trace the origin. At first I thought she was hurt, then lifted my hand and saw it was my blood.

Chapter Thirty

In the brick-lined stable courtyard, a groom met us to show Night to her stall. Victoria led the mare into the stables while I stood rooted to the bricks. Ivy covered one wall of the brick and fieldstone enclosure. Tall, airy locust trees shaded the yard. Shiny, contented horses gazed indifferently at us over their stall doors, and I at them.

The overwhelmingly powerful desire I'd felt to beat Georgia into a lifeless pulp was slow to leave. I felt the tension in my muscles, as though they knew independently that they had not finished the job. My body felt composed of a pack of hunting wolves, thwarted from their kill.

Each breath I took was conscious, drawn slowly in to fill lungs, the air released from my body carrying fragments of Jane. I tried to not let them escape, worried all of my memories of her would slip away on the wind.

I felt the weight of my body on my feet, standing on the bricks in the courtyard. The weight was illusionary. I imagined particles of myself evaporating on the air, like Jane, until no one was there.

Isadora Chamberlain arrived from the house, and I introduced Victoria Branch as Night's owner and Jane's best friend. Isadora gazed at me, slightly raising her eyebrows, but turned before I could question her. I wondered what she'd left unsaid.

We followed her through a small wooden plank door in the brick wall, passing into a beautiful, aromatic herb garden. I closed my eyes for a moment, and for the first time the breath coming in to me carried something of its own. The scent of sage, warm from the sun, caressed the air around me. I came to a sudden halt, arrested by the strong pull of home.

Reluctantly, I went through a recessed door that led into the house. All I wanted at that moment was to be home, and the herb garden seemed the closest thing. When we entered the house, I again felt that odd detachment of no past and no future. The scent of sage had briefly connected me with my past. I didn't want to enter the future. The brick-floored room leading off the garden room had sinks and counters for cutting and arranging flowers. Various tweed jackets, some with leather elbow patches, hung on hooks along the hall.

New England Butch.

We went up a flight of stone stairs, worn slightly in the center. I knew each person who had climbed these steps had added to the depression, taking a fragment of the stone on their feet. At the top, Isadora held the door open for us to enter a main hall tiled with black and white parquet. Off to the side, I got a glimpse of a formal room with uninviting furniture. Eighteenth-century hunting prints hung on the walls. We walked straight past to a cozy-overstuffed-chair sort of room.

The paintings on these walls were horses, but the brush was modern. Vivid, spirited, lively colors brought out the joy horses give us. Victoria and I sat near each other on a sofa, our loss keeping us close. A woman in slacks brought in a teapot with pastries on a tray. I watched her and Isadora and found their relationship polite, but casual. It occurred to me that both the groom and the refreshments had been called up by cell phone en route. Isadora had made another call, she explained. "I took the liberty of telephoning the county sheriff's office, requesting they send someone around. But in the meantime, I'd like to hear your story."

A Norwich terrier jumped into her lap. Isadora pulled him close and stroked his wiry coat.

"I thought all the horse people in the east are required to own a Jack Russell terrier," I said. "Part of the uniform."

"My dear, I never pay any attention to what others do." Something in her smile told me we were sisters.

"Thank you, Dorothy." She smiled at the woman serving us, waiting for her to leave the room and close the door. Her gaze came back to us. "Don't leave anything out."

"The trouble began when Megan Fisk, a woman who trained with Georgia Farmer, died. Georgia trains horses and coaches..." I struggled to line out all the words enough to make sense.

Isadora nodded briskly. "I know about Georgia." She wasn't smiling. "That young woman training with her was worth a hundred of her. Tell me what you think happened."

I told her about finding the electric cord in Georgia's garden shed, and related its use.

Now Isadora was downright frowning. "Think she was in the business of killing horses for profit?"

That stopped me cold. "Maybe," I said. "But I think this was more personal, a crime of passion, not cold-blooded business. She believed she blended in with a certain class of horse people, and no one would ever suspect that class of horrible doings."

"Or being queer," Isadora said with a straight face but a twinkle in her eyes.

I gave her a slow nod. "Georgia thought she was a white horse in winter."

"Ah. A passing woman. But the snow all melted away, and then she was exposed." Isadora looked hard at me.

"That's right," I said. "That fear drove her, the fear of exposure of her gayness, of her lowly working-class family. It isolated her and made her a lonely, desperate woman."

"I know Georgia thought she successfully hid her lesbianism," Isadora said dryly. "She would absolutely disintegrate if she realized how widespread the knowledge was." She gave a short bark of a laugh.

Victoria shifted on the couch. "Jane told me Georgia worried all the time about people finding out, and what it would do to her training business. I think, even beyond losing the income, her main concern was losing the Pony Club following. They've been meeting there as long as she has been in business. Poor thing, to live in fear of such exposure," Victoria said.

"Poor thing be damned. I never entirely trust people who have something they believe needs to be hidden." Isadora set her teacup down with a crisp clink into the saucer on the table beside her.

"I know things have changed in the last few years, but it can't be that easy to be gay in a homophobic world," Vic said. "Look what's happening in Russia."

"Oh, Ms. Chamberlain knows," I said, holding Isadora's gaze.

"You are right, dear. And I cannot tolerate the twisted behavior of homophobes, queer or straight." Isadora shifted her dog and crossed her booted ankles.

Isadora was done with Georgia. "Tell me about your relationships to each other. Vic?"

Victoria answered, "I'd say I'm happily married to my husband, except it is one of the more obnoxious things straight women can say. But no, my relationship with Jane was one of longtime loving friendship."

A soft knock on the door interrupted this moment. The door opened a bit. "Ms. Chamberlain, the police are here."

Two men entered, crossing the oriental carpet as though it were strewn with eggshells. One was John, the Amherst chief of police, the other one a state police detective who showed his badge and introduced himself. They both sat and looked attentive.

"Now," said the chief, "perhaps you could fill us in on all the details leading up to today."

I opened my mouth to tell the whole sordid story and found I had no voice. I looked at Vic, and she caught the ball. Victoria did a great job laying out all the facts and history of the events. I sat there and numbed myself so I couldn't hear or think about losing Jane. Once in a while I tuned in and just as quickly checked back out.

"I don't get it," the detective said. "You say that Ms. Farmer switched the horses and made it look as if the dead horse was the valuable one?"

"Yes," I broke in. "I had a rush DNA profile done on the living horse, which proved it was the one Megan planned on taking to the Olympics. Georgia was listed as co-owner and was slated to collect seventy-five thousand on the horse's death. The second string horse was the one she killed. A ringer. And I think she killed her father who worked there as a groom because he knew the true identity of the horses."

"Wasn't that death listed as an accident?"

"Yes, but if you press her, she may admit it. She has nothing to lose now," Victoria said.

"She was savagely sexually abused by her father and later kept him around so she could get revenge." I had no compunctions about telling Georgia's secret.

"The papers reported Megan was found with a syringe in her hand. What do you think was in it?" the state guy asked me directly.

I opened my mouth and croaked. Cleared my throat and said, "The bottle for the drug Georgia used on Jane was right there. Somulose is a common drug for equine euthanasia. My guess is that she had a stock of it. Probably stolen from a veterinarian's office."

The two police officers looked at each other, then one turned to me and said, "There was a break-in at Green Mountain Equine hospital over a year ago. Three bottles of that drug were taken along with other drugs. We'd given up on tracking them."

"It's been too long ago to prove anything, but the mink farm guys who picked the horse up believe the horse wasn't euthanized with drugs. They claim Georgia told them it had been 'accidentally' electrocuted."

"The syringe may have been used legitimately at some time to destroy a sick or injured horse, then kept sealed in a bag," Vic speculated.

The detective raised his eyebrows at her. He looked unsmiling around the room at all of us. "I don't get the motivation."

"Megan had decided to take her horse to a different trainer," I said.

"So?"

"She had also threatened to out Georgia."

"Out?"

At the detective's puzzled face, Isadora said, "To expose her sexual orientation."

Slowly a dim light came on in the detective's eyes, glowing brighter. "So, this was blackmail?"

"No one was trying to blackmail Georgia, although she stood to gain quite a lot of money on the insured death of the horse. The only person who cared about her sexual orientation was Georgia. Her fear of being exposed was part of what drove her to kill two people and attempt a third. Me. After Jane died, I wanted to wipe that woman off the face of the earth." I felt my breath come faster and the color rise in my face as I spoke. Then I folded. "I should have done something to stop her."

"That's ridiculous," Vic cried.

"I could have stopped her from injecting Jane." I couldn't go on.

"Now, Miles," Ms. Chamberlain said. "You can't dwell on that. You did your best to save her. Georgia's intentions were clear."

"Georgia Farmer has been transported to the hospital. She claims you tried to kill her."

"I did."

"She's a hurting piece of human being. Madder than hell and accusing you of, um, lots of crimes."

"The day started with me being hit over the head by Georgia, handcuffed with those plastic things, and dragged into one of Georgia's horse stalls."

The detective, Chuck, was skeptical. "Can you tell me how you got out of handcuffs?"

"I escaped and got a lift here with a bunch of girls on their way to North Hampton."

"But how, exactly?"

I barked a short laugh. "Wasn't too hard. I found a box of matches in my jeans. Jane and I had burned leaves at her place a couple of days ago." I had to be careful to keep away from that memory.

"How did you get out of them?" asked John.

I realized that no one had heard this story other than the car full of wild gals.

"Well, as I said, I had that little box of matches." I told the story.

"That's not possible, to melt them off," John interrupted.

"You'll find what's left of them in the fourth stall down from the office. The one with the wheelbarrow parked under the hay drop. That's how I climbed out."

John stood up and walked over to me, "I still don't understand how."

He took both my hands and pushed the sleeves up. I winced. He untied the hankie and gently peeled the shredded gloves off.

"Oh. I see." He raised his eyes to mine. "You need a doctor."

This propelled Vic and Isadora out of their seats and into a tight circle around my wrists.

CHAPTER THIRTY-ONE

That evening I packed my bag, with Vic's help. The bandages they put on at the hospital wrapped my wrist, crossing my palms with just the ends of my fingers sticking out. I had told Vic earlier, "Jane's absence is too raw. There's no way I can stay in her house. Would you mind putting up with me?"

"Absolutely. I'll take Scout out while you pack."

But once the bags were packed and I had paced through the house, ostensibly looking for strewn belongings like socks but soaking up the last of Jane's home, her space, all that was left, I thought differently. "Look, I can't leave here right now. Do you mind if I change my mind, maybe drive over to your place later? Tomorrow?"

"That's fine. You can spend Sunday with us. Your plane leaves at six on Monday morning. We'll have to leave the house by two thirty in the gawd-awful morning."

Scout jumped on the bed to curl up beside my duffel bag.

"What will happen to her now?"

Vic looked startled. "Scout? I don't know. We can't take her. Or any dog. My husband's allergic."

We looked at each other, the quandary almost palpable. Scout had not only lost her person, she would lose her familiar home as well. All the haunts, her routine, the places she liked to sniff and scratch.

"What'll be done with the horses? Can you find some situation for them?"

"I'll work on it. My daughter has always lusted after Dusty." Vic sighed. "Well, try to be at my place by four o'clock. Sunday dinner." She walked over to the place where Jane hung her keys, sorted out a set and handed them to me. "Here are the extra car keys."

Before she closed the door, she poked her head back in and said, "You sure you'll be all right? If you change your mind, just come over."

"Love you, Vic."

"You, too."

Vic shut the door, and I watched her pass the windows on the way to her car. With the fading of the engine sounds, the house returned to its normal quiet.

The telephone rang. The sound jabbed me like an electric current shooting off the squat black phone. I didn't care who it was. I wasn't about to explain to some stranger that Jane was dead. When it had quit ringing, I picked up the receiver and punched in my own number. Tess answered. I had to cough a few times to clear my throat. "How is everything? Good. Just want you to know I'll be back day after tomorrow. I've got a four-hour layover in Salt Lake and a three-hour wait in Minneapolis. Can you pick me up in Helena about seven thirty? How's Burt?"

"He's right here," Tess said.

"Wait!" I shouted into the phone and Tess came back. "I have something to tell you, so after I've spoken with Burt, let's talk a minute."

"Okay, Miles," Tess said. "Here's your sis."

"Hi, sis. You almost home soon? We are sitting down to dinner right now."

"Soon. Did you cook?"

Burt whispered into the phone. "Tess doesn't like me to use the oven."

I laughed. "When I get back, we'll go shopping together and you can pick out some new things to make. How's that mare? Alec."

"She's really nice. Talks to me a lot."

"Does she say when she's dropping her colt?"

"She's ready anytime. Bye, sis."

"Bye, Burt," I said, but he'd already hung up.

I had to call again so I could tell Tess about what happened. I ended with, "I'll be arriving in poor shape."

"Oh, Miles, I'm so sorry. It all sounds dreadful."

After I disconnected, I realized that I'd called home to ground myself. That was where I belonged. I went through the kitchen to go outside, stand and breathe.

The horses called, so I took Scout out to the barn, and I dropped down some hay. Scout went for a mouse behind the wheelbarrow. I sat on one of the snack bales and listened to the horses chewing.

Chrysanthemums musked the air. The same airborne scent both Jane and her father had breathed in. Now they were gone. My mind touched on the belief of spirits living on, of life after death, whatever the hell that meant. Maybe it was as simple as inhaling particles of flowers.

Shadows lengthened. I turned my head to look at the dark, empty house. "Come on, Scout." She wiggled, ran ahead. I thought she'd go to the back door, as always, but she trotted out to the driveway and sat looking up the road.

"She's not coming...ever." I said the first part all right,

but when I got to "ever," my voice broke, and the last word was a whisper.

My legs buckled, and I sank down to my knees onto the gravel. "Scout, stop waiting."

Scout ignored me and settled down under the locust trees in her vigil.

On a long rasping exhale, my body folded over at the waist, and I rested my forehead on the sharp stones. The sounds that came out of my body were strangers and so far removed from human that I scared myself.

The fact I was alone for the first time since Jane had died made it possible to simply be guttural, let the snot run along with the horrible sense of loss. I howled and cried the cold dark night down like a blanket of death.

I lay there after a while, curled up on my side, spent of my tears. The full dark of night pooled over me, shrouding me from the world. Scout touched me with her cold nose, followed by a quick lick. I shoved myself to my knees and looked at the dog, who went back to her waiting position in the driveway. Went into the house and turned on some lamps. Thought about building a fire in the fireplace. Didn't.

Sitting on the couch, I could almost feel her on the cushions beside me. I closed my eyes. The house gave off little creaks and rustles, the way an old house does. Echoes of energy from the lives lived inside. With my eyes closed, I could almost feel Jane moving around her home.

After a while I got up, went to the door, and called the dog. She wouldn't come, so I went out and picked her up, carried her to the kitchen. "You've got to be hungry." She looked up at me with her brown eyes, turned and lay down in front of the door, nose at the jamb. I mixed some food for her and set it on the tiles. She ignored it.

"I'm not hungry, either."

I drifted through the house, from room to room, both putting off and longing for the smell of the sheets.

CHAPTER THIRTY-TWO

Sometime in the night, the little dog had jumped on the bed and curled up along my legs. Her gentle snoring lulled me. At first light, lying there with my eyes wide open, I thought I smelled coffee brewing. The powerful image I had wanted to remember came back in a rush, of Jane carrying two cups of coffee into the bedroom, slipping off her robe. The curve and swing of her breasts.

This memory, the scent of her on the sheets, and my imagining the coffee were too much. I shot my legs out of the covers and went to the kitchen. Stopped in my tracks. Coffee was brewing; it wasn't my imagination. Dumbfounded, I stared at the pot gurgling on the counter, like it must posses Jane in its interior. The damned thing had a timer, and my efficient darling had set it before we left for Quail Mountain.

I showered, dressed in clean clothes, and drank some coffee, all on autopilot. In the file cabinet, I found the manila envelope Jane and I had prepared. I dug out Scout's shot records and went out to the barn to locate her shipping crate.

I tossed some hay to the horses and stood with the pitchfork in my hand watching them, like a Grant Wood painting. Life gets strange when you start thinking of every motion, each act as "the last time."

By nine that morning, I drove into Victoria's driveway.

"You're early."

"Couldn't take it anymore." I told her about the coffee.

Vic just nodded, slowly.

"Come on, I'll see what's around for breakfast."

"I'm not hungry."

"You have to eat."

"Neither is Scout."

Victoria poured me a cup of coffee. "Everything has been happening too fast. There is one problem I can put you at ease about. The horses. My daughter would love to have Dusty, and my husband and I talked about this last night. He'll add on to the barn, put in a loafing shed for the blind mare and her companion."

"Good. Dusty's a horse who will be happiest with a teenage girl."

Later, a knock on the door woke the little dog sleeping on my lap. She ran wildly barking for the door.

The chief of police loomed in the doorway. "You mind if I come in to bring you up to date on this affair?"

"Please do." Vic indicated a chair.

Before he sat, he looked at me and said, "It has been confirmed. Ms. Scott died from an injection of Somulose. The coroner believes the drug would have been administered intramuscularly. It is supposed to be put into a vein."

"When I first found the car, Jane was kicking the trunk lid. I thought she'd been gagged, but she hadn't been. Not when I found her later, anyway."

The police officer picked at the edge of his hat for a moment, then looked up and met my eyes. "Intramuscular injections of that drug can cause convulsions."

I squeezed my brain empty. Later. I'd deal with this later.

He sat down with a groan. "Just wanted you folks to know

everything checked out. Got a little bonus. We opened Arthur's safe deposit box. He kept a detailed diary. He wrote that he wanted to destroy Georgia for killing Wyatt. On top of that, he claimed she had killed his wife, her own mother, after driving him out of the household. See, her parents got a divorce and immediately after it was final, the girl and her mother took a road trip out west."

"She killed her own mother at the age of nineteen? That is just too sordid." Victoria shook her head as though trying to expel the idea from her mind.

I cleared my voice. "The mother enabled her husband's sexual abuse of her daughter for years. Georgia must have seethed because her mother looked the other way. She got them both in the end, and enough money to buy a horse facility that would propel her to the top." I handed him the manila envelope Jane and I had put together. "You'll find it all laid out here. I sent off for DNA confirmation, proof that Georgia switched the horses, and a description of how to use an electric wire for killing a horse. You'll find Georgia's device hanging in her garage. At least I hope so. I took a picture of it hanging in place, and that's in the envelope. Also a narrative in chronological order of what Jane and I believed happened."

He read the writing on the front, "In the event of..." He looked at me.

"We were afraid something might happen to us."

Victoria wiped her hand across her forehead, as though trying to evict the poison. "When you interviewed Georgia, did she say anything about her own lesbianism?"

"No. She adamantly denied that she was, as she said, perverted. Claimed Jane Scott tried to seduce her." He looked at me, a worried frown making me realize my rising anger was showing.

"I should have killed her."

The policeman frowned. "Well, that might be a problem. She claims you did try and filed an assault claim. I will need you to come to the office to make and sign a statement. There may be court proceedings."

"I don't believe it! What about what she did to Miles?" Victoria looked outraged.

"I can come in today, but I must go back home to deal with things on the ranch, round up cows, and drive them out of the mountains before hunting season starts. My brother is developmentally disabled, and he can't manage alone. So I will have to make some arrangements and then come back. But I have to tell you, there's no way I have the money to fly out here again. Look, what about doing the interview at our sheriff's office? They have the video equipment. Is there a way that might work out? I have a ticket to fly home tomorrow morning. Early."

"Let me check with the county attorney. We may be able to set up a Skype call for him to be present. You may be required to post a bond. Under the circumstances," he glanced at my wrists, "he might make an exception."

Victoria said, "Why don't you open the file right now, then if you have any questions Miles can answer them."

The officer opened the thick manila envelope, drawing out the five pages relating the events as we had laid them out, plus all the Warmblood registry related papers, safe deposit key, and a slim, white envelope. It was blank.

The policeman opened it, pulled out a single sheet of paper and read off, "Jane Scott, my last will and testament." After reading another line silently, he raised his gaze to the two women and said, "Maybe you should have Ms. Scott's lawyer read this."

"I'm sure she will," Victoria said, absently. "Why are you concerned?"

"She left her house and contents to you," he said, nodding in Vic's direction. "Then after all the legal language it says, 'Becky Miles gets all the candy.'"

Pain came in a flood, along every vein from all the capillaries, like ice water to my core.

CHAPTER THIRTY-THREE

Vic gave me the facts of Jane's financial picture, now mine, on the way to the airport the next morning.

"Jane was always very open with me about her money, how she invested it and where she made her donations. Everything is invested, of course. The yearly income from the investments alone is one hundred thousand. You'll need to get a good accountant and a wealth management consultant."

"Right. I haven't a clue."

"Changes things a bit, doesn't it?"

"You bet. Always, there's a nagging worry that calf prices will go down, or I'll have a rain-spoiled hay crop, or some vital piece of equipment will need replacing. Why on earth did she leave it to me, Vic? I don't get it."

"I knew she planned on doing this, knowing how quickly things can change and people can die. I think she wanted you to experience the freedom of not having to worry about money. We don't want it to influence us, but it does, either having it or not."

"I don't know what to say. Do you know when she set this up?"

"A couple of months ago, at least. But she must have consulted a lawyer recently. Don't forget, she lost both parents in the flash of an instant. She didn't want any hassle for you, so she made it very legal."

"I am so happy she left you her beautiful house, the gardens and barn. Her place is a gem. What will you do with it? Would you live there?"

"Strange. Michael and I have begun talking about downsizing our house now that the children are on the verge of adulthood. They both have colleges lined up. I can think of no more beautiful place to live." Vic was silent a moment. "Or my ashes to rest. That line in the will, she wanted her ashes spread among the iris in the garden."

"Yes. Her father's garden. She must have been very close to him."

Vic left the highway on the ramp to the airport.

"I'm relieved you'll be there," I said. "So much of Jane is in that house, now I can imagine her closest friend moving through the rooms."

"I'll call a real estate agent when I get back today. Put our place on the market. I don't want Jane's place to be empty for long." Vic's voice trailed into silence. She made no effort to fill the space. Vic walked into the airport with me, aimlessly wandering to the check-in area with red eyes. "Let's try to find some drinkable coffee."

We both bought fancy coffee at a Starbucks booth and sat away from other people while we quietly drank the hot brew. Each of us moved like robots. After drinking the coffee, we chucked the cups in the waste bin, then proceeded to the Delta counter, pushing a luggage cart with Scout's crate to the baggage check area.

Victoria gave me a long hug. I did one of those gasps you do when you are trying like hell not to sob. Well, maybe on second thought, it was a sob.

Once I got the pain in my chest under control, I said to

Vic, "You're going to have a tougher time. Everything around Putney will remind you of her and times you spent together."

Neither one of us said anything. Her eyes were swimming in tears, but otherwise she looked the way she always did. Vic gave me a little squeeze on my biceps, turned and walked away.

Many hours later, I walked into the arms of Tess and my brother, who was so happy to see me and had no idea why Tess and I were crying. I just didn't want to ever tell him about Jane. His sense of safety and permanence had already been shaken.

"I brought back something from the East," I said, walking to baggage claim.

"What?" My brother went through a long list of anything he imagined might be arriving on the conveyor belt. "Lobster? Maple syrup? Holstein cow?" He laughed at that one.

The big dog crate came bumping along. Inside was a wiggling Scout, so happy to see me. I let her out and snapped a leash on her collar.

Norburt reached out to pet her, quickly drawing his hand back. "She's all rough."

"Her coat is a lot different from our border collies. She's going to live with us."

Norburt gave me a tepid half smile. "Okay. If you say so."

On the way to the car, he said, "That sorrel mare has been pacing all morning."

"Really? She's only been bagging up for two weeks. You think she's close?"

"I think she's tired of it," Norburt said.

Tess and I laughed. Tess said, "Well, ask any woman who has given birth, and I think she'll agree with you."

Burt smiled with delight. "I was right, huh?"

Nothing on earth is like the first sight of home again after being away on a traumatic journey. The dogs yipped and ran in circles. Skipper sat right in front of me with her front paws on my toes, her butt wiggling in the dirt. I ruffled her silky ears, looked into her mismatched eyes, and told her how much I'd missed her. "I brought you a new buddy." I opened the car door and Scout jumped out. From then on, the three dogs were wrapped up in each other.

When I waved good-bye and thanked Tess beaucoup, I thought I needed to come up with something she'd really like. Maybe I should get out my leather tools and make her a saddle. A nice basket weave across the fenders and skirt. The winter would be a long one, and I'd welcome something to do.

"Burt, I'm going to look at Alec. Want to come?"

"Sure, sis."

Alec was indeed close. I bent down to see her udder and it had a shiny gloss, the teats filled. Her vulva was soft and draped in long folds, her front feet treading the straw. "You're right, Burt. She could foal at any time."

The mare had been well cared for and had actually gained a little weight. "She looks good. What are you feeding her, Burt?"

"All the hay she wants, just like you said. In the morning she gets a can of that rolled oats sweet feed, for lunch the hot bran mash, and dinner another can of sweet feed." Burt looked at his shoes. "I give her carrots before I go to bed. I hope that's all right."

"Yes. I'll bet she likes them."

"She eats them all up. Alec is a nice horse, and she likes me."

That night I went to bed about eight, my body thinking it was ten. Set the alarm for midnight to check on the mare. She seemed restless, but no more so than earlier. At two in the morning it was the same, but at four, she had dark sweat marks along her neck and flanks. I went into the stall and saw one little hoof sticking out.

I hustled to the tack room where I had my obstetrics equipment for calving. Reaching for the chains, I saw my bandaged hands and knew the gauze would have to come off in order to get the latex gloves on. I grabbed the edge of the tape with my teeth and yanked. I finished the job with scissors, and I was pleased to see that in only a few days my cut palm was well on the way to healing. Didn't look at the burns.

When I got back to the stall, she was flat on her side, pushing hard. After a grunt, she stopped pushing and lay there panting. I waited for her to get going again, but she stayed down. I opened the stall door and moved around behind her. Alec weakly lifted her head when I came into the stall, then let it fall back with a thud.

Lying down by her tail, I saw that after all that work there was only one foot, and pulled on an obstetrics glove. I slipped my hand past the tiny foot and felt the other hoof at about halfway up the birth canal, the nose nestled in between the legs. I sighed with relief. Normal presentation. The reason this little colt didn't just pop out was the weakness of the mare.

Unfolding the towel to expose the obstetrics chains, I slid one end of the chain into the mare and around the far leg, the other end wrapped around the exposed hoof. I sat up, bracing one foot on the mare's lower rump, and set up a gentle traction, hoping this would stimulate her to go back into labor.

It worked. She pushed. A little halfheartedly, but she pushed, and I drew a little harder on the chains. She stopped and went limp, and I waited for her to regain some strength. Now the deepest hoof was exposed, and the little nose was at the opening.

The widest part of the foal, the shoulders and chest, were at the cervical opening. She lay quietly until I began to get concerned. I gave a little tug to remind her that she had a job ahead. A strong contraction took hold, and the mare's feet came up off the straw. I pulled as hard as I thought I could, and suddenly the foal slipped through the cervix and was mostly out on the straw. I removed the chains, cleared away the white sac from the foal's head, and waited for the blood to go from the placenta to the baby in the last surge from the umbilical cord.

The foal raised its black head like a drunkard. The front feet moved. This movement seemed to galvanize Alec, like she suddenly realized something alive was back there. She climbed to her feet and spun around nickering to her foal, who gave a funny little humph back. The cord broke when the mare stood, but it had been plenty of time for the foal to get all the blood from the placenta.

Curious about the gender, I lifted the wobbling critter's tail and discovered it was a filly. I always liked fillies. After dousing the broken end of the umbilical cord in iodine, I crawled back to the wall of the stall and watched the show.

I'd never seen such a small baby horse before. I guess some of it had to do with the breed. Arabians are smaller than quarter horses, but also the lack of prenatal nutrition for the fetus must have a lot to do with it.

Alec, meanwhile, was giving her baby a bath, rasping off the amniotic fluid, stimulating the little being to rise to her feet. With a big jerk, the black filly almost propelled herself to her feet and went down in a nosedive just as fast. The second time she stayed, shaking and gazing all around. Alec nearly knocked her down with her welcome licking. Pretty soon I heard the wonderful sucking slurping noises of the first feeding. I rose to my feet, collected the calving chains and towel, and dropped them off in the tack room on my way to make a bran mash and a cup of coffee in the house.

When the kettle was full, I set it over the gas ring, lifting off the whistle. A strong cup of coffee in one hand and the bucket with the mash in the other, I returned to the barn. While I'd been gone, Alec had passed the placenta. I lifted it up with the manure fork and spread it out in the aisle to make sure it was all there. Didn't want a torn-off piece left inside her to fester. The foal's eleven-month-old home looked in great shape. I slipped it into a feedbag and placed it by the barn door, then returned to my coffee and the show the new foal was providing.

I thought about how different my life would be from what both Jane and I had hoped. How can time and space be empty? I thought about her will and the fact she'd made it way before I even made the trip out to Vermont. I didn't know how it would feel to never have to worry about money again, the deep-down relief of that. Somehow, Jane had understood. The place that held the relief also held the grief.

I crossed the deep straw of the stall to the open half door to Alec's corral. I leaned one elbow heavily on the top of the door, rubbing my eyes. Across the valley, a sliver of morning edged the horizon.

Going out the main barn doors, I called Scout and Skip to come with me. Something about a new foal entering the world filled me with a wash of feelings, too many to name. I couldn't stand the confinement of walls and roof right then.

❖

The sound of the brass zipper closing my ranch jacket was loud on the night air. I walked farther out into the sagebrush and grass, rattling dry with approaching winter. I took a deep breath to filter the clean air, washed by mountain winds, through my nostrils. I was far from the stink of cities. My boot soles crunched over the carpet of dry, yellow grass and scraped across prickly pear. The blue-black sky, packed from horizon to mountain edge with stars, formed my limitless ceiling. Sage scent surrounded me, clean and musky. A whiff of juniper rode the wind, a tantalizing reminder of smoke from a campfire. I closed my eyes to feel the endless space reaching out beneath my boots, arching over my head. The sounds of Scout and Skipper chasing some imagined thing through the brush made me smile. Those two had hit it off like old buds. Murna was a mite jealous, but she'd get over that.

A gust of chill wind slapped my jeans against my legs. I lifted the sheepskin collar, tilted my head back, and entered the stars. The wind circled round me, caressing my cheek, my lips, and holding me in a loose corral.

About the Author

Franci McMahon brings together the world of horses and lesbians. Her first novel, *Staying The Distance*, was published by Firebrand. She is pleased to have her second novel, along with the sequel, published by Bold Strokes Books. She has many works in anthologies, stories for children and adults in national magazines, and a poetry prize, and she had an enriching stay at Hedgebrook.

The double granddaughter of Western pioneers, she grew up in sage country. Classical music and Patsy Cline, riding a good horse herding cows to the high country, cooking, reading complex novels with a story, dancing close to a warm woman, and sitting in silence often at Quaker meetings are some of her deepest pleasures. She divides her time between Montana and Tucson, Arizona.

Books Available From Bold Strokes Books

Deadly Medicine by Jaime Maddox. Dr. Ward Thrasher's life is in turmoil. Her partner Jess left her, and her job puts her in the path of a murderous physician who has Jess in his sights. (978-1-62639-4-247)

New Beginnings by KC Richardson. Can the connection and attraction between Jordan Roberts and Kirsten Murphy be enough for Jordan to trust Kirsten with her heart? (978-1-62639-4-506)

Officer Down by Erin Dutton. Can two women who've made careers out of being there for others in crisis find the strength to need each other? (978-1-62639-4-230)

Reasonable Doubt by Carsen Taite. Just when Sarah and Ellery think they've left dangerous careers behind, a new case sets them—and their hearts—on a collision course. (978-1-62639-4-421)

Tarnished Gold by Ann Aptaker. Cantor Gold must outsmart the Law, outrun New York's dockside gangsters, outplay a shady art dealer, his lover, and a beautiful curator, and stay out of a killer's gun sights. (978-1-62639-4-261)

The Renegade by Amy Dunne. Post-apocalyptic survivors Alex and Evelyn secretly find love while held captive by a deranged cult, but when their relationship is discovered, they must fight for their freedom—or die trying. (978-1-62639-4-278)

Thrall by Barbara Ann Wright. Four women in a warrior society must work together to lift an insidious curse while caught between their own desires, the will of their peoples, and an ancient evil. (978-1-62639-4-377)

White Horse in Winter by Franci McMahon. Love between two women collides with the inner poison of a closeted horse trainer in the green hills of Vermont. (978-1-62639-4-292)

Autumn Spring by Shelley Thrasher. Can Bree and Linda, two women in the autumn of their lives, put their hearts first and find the love they've never dared seize? (978-1-62639-365-3)

The Chameleon's Tale by Andrea Bramhall. Two old friends must work through a web of lies and deceit to find themselves again, but in the search they discover far more than they ever went looking for. (978-1-62639-363-9)

Side Effects by VK Powell. Detective Jordan Bishop and Dr. Neela Sahjani must decide if it's easier to trust someone with your heart or your life as they face threatening protestors, corrupt politicians, and their increasing attraction. (978-1-62639-364-6)

Warm November by Kathleen Knowles. What do you do if the one woman you want is the only one you can't have? (978-1-62639-366-0)

In Every Cloud by Tina Michele. When Bree finally leaves her shattered life behind, is she strong enough to salvage the remaining pieces of her heart and find the place where it truly fits? (978-1-62639-413-1)

Rise of the Gorgon by Tanai Walker. When independent Internet journalist Elle Pharell goes to Kuwait to investigate a veteran's mysterious suicide, she hires Cassandra Hunt, an interpreter with a covert agenda. (978-1-62639-367-7)

Crossed by Meredith Doench. Agent Luce Hansen returns home to catch a killer and risks everything to revisit the unsolved murder of her first girlfriend and confront the demons of her youth. (978-1-62639-361-5)

Making a Comeback by Julie Blair. Music and love take center stage when jazz pianist Liz Randall tries to make a comeback with the help of her reclusive, blind neighbor, Jac Winters. (978-1-62639-357-8)

Soul Unique by Gun Brooke. Self-proclaimed cynic Greer Landon falls for Hayden Rowe's paintings and the young woman shortly after, but will Hayden, who lives with Asperger syndrome, trust her and reciprocate her feelings? (978-1-62639-358-5)

The Price of Honor by Radclyffe. Honor and duty are not always black and white—and when self-styled patriots take up arms against the government, the price of honor may be a life. (978-1-62639-359-2)

Mounting Evidence by Karis Walsh. Lieutenant Abigail Hargrove and her mounted police unit need to solve a murder and protect wetland biologist Kira Lovell during the Washington State Fair. (978-1-62639-343-1)

Threads of the Heart by Jeannie Levig. Maggie and Addison Rae-McInnis share a love and a life, but are the threads that bind them together strong enough to withstand Addison's restlessness and the seductive Victoria Fontaine? (978-1-62639-410-0)

Sheltered Love by MJ Williamz. Boone Fairway and Grey Dawson—two women touched by abuse—overcome their pasts to find happiness in each other. (978-1-62639-362-2)

Searching for Celia by Elizabeth Ridley. As American spy novelist Dayle Salvesen investigates the mysterious disappearance of her ex-lover, Celia, in London, she begins questioning how well she knew Celia—and how well she knows herself. (978-1-62639-356-1).

Hardwired by C.P. Rowlands. Award-winning teacher Clary Stone and Leefe Ellis, manager of the homeless shelter for small children, stand together in a part of Clary's hometown that she never knew existed. (978-1-62639-351-6)

The Muse by Meghan O'Brien. Erotica author Kate McMannis struggles with writer's block until a gorgeous muse entices her into a world of fantasy sex and inadvertent romance. (978-1-62639-223-6)

Death's Doorway by Crin Claxton. Helping the dead can be deadly: Tony may be listening to the dead, but she needs to learn to listen to the living. (978-1-62639-354-7)

No Good Reason by Cari Hunter. A violent kidnapping in a Peak District village pushes Detective Sanne Jensen and lifelong friend Dr. Meg Fielding closer, just as it threatens to tear everything apart. (978-1-62639-352-3)

The 45th Parallel by Lisa Girolami. Burying her mother isn't the worst thing that can happen to Val Montague when she returns to the woodsy but peculiar town of Hemlock, Oregon. (978-1-62639-342-4)

Romance by the Book by Jo Victor. If Cam didn't keep disrupting her life, maybe Alex could uncover the secret of a century-old love story, and solve the greatest mystery of all—her own heart. (978-1-62639-353-0)

A Royal Romance by Jenny Frame. In a country where class still divides, can love topple the last social taboo and allow Queen Georgina and Beatrice Elliot, a working-class girl, their happy ever after? (978-1-62639-360-8)

Bouncing by Jaime Maddox. Basketball coach Alex Dalton has been bouncing from woman to woman because no one ever held her interest, until she meets her new assistant, Britain Dodge. (978-1-62639-344-8)

Same Time Next Week by Emily Smith. A chance encounter between Alex Harris and the beautiful Michelle Masters leads to a whirlwind friendship and causes Alex to question everything she's ever known—including her own marriage. (978-1-62639-345-5)

All Things Rise by Missouri Vaun. Cole rescues a striking pilot who crash-lands near her family's farm, setting in motion a chain of events that will forever alter the course of her life. (978-1-62639-346-2)

Riding Passion by D. Jackson Leigh. Mount up for the ride through a sizzling anthology of chance encounters, buried desires, romantic surprises, and blazing passion. (978-1-62639-349-3)

Love's Bounty by Yolanda Wallace. Lobster boat captain Jake Myers stopped living the day she cheated death, but meeting greenhorn Shy Silva stirs her back to life. (978-1-62639334-9)

Just Three Words by Melissa Brayden. Sometimes the one you want is the one you least suspect…Accountant Samantha Ennis has her ordered life disrupted when heartbreaker Hunter Blair moves into her trendy Soho loft. (978-1-62639-335-6)

Lay Down the Law by Carsen Taite. Attorney Peyton Davis returns to her Texas roots to take on big oil and the Mexican Mafia, but will her investigation thwart her chance at true love? (978-1-62639-336-3)

Playing in Shadow by Lesley Davis. Survivor's guilt threatens to keep Bryce trapped in her nightmare world unless Scarlet's love can pull her out of the darkness back into the light. (978-1-62639-337-0)

Soul Selecta by Gill McKnight. Soul mates are hell to work with. (978-1-62639-338-7)

Shadow Hunt by L.L. Raand. With young to raise and her Pack under attack, Sylvan, Alpha of the wolf Weres, takes on her greatest challenge when she determines to uncover the faceless enemies known as the Shadow Lords. A Midnight Hunters novel. (978-1-62639-326-4)

Heart of the Game by Rachel Spangler. A baseball writer falls for a single mom, but can she ever love anything as much as she loves the game? (978-1-62639-327-1)

Prayer of the Handmaiden by Merry Shannon. Celibate priestess Kadrian must defend the kingdom of Ithyria from a dangerous enemy and ultimately choose between her duty to the Goddess and the love of her childhood sweetheart, Erinda. (978-1-62639-329-5)

The Witch of Stalingrad by Justine Saracen. A Soviet "night witch" pilot and American journalist meet on the Eastern Front in WWII and struggle through carnage, conflicting politics, and the deadly Russian winter. (978-1-62639-330-1)

Lightning Source UK Ltd.
Milton Keynes UK
UKOW04f0831270915

259327UK00001B/19/P

9 781626 394292